The Trailer Park

The Woods

Andy's House

The Big House

Pappa Joe and
Nini's House

The Fort

The Cliffs

The Tracks

The Graveyard

The School

The Town

Kennedy's Store

The Big House

The Big House

by Robert Vasvary

© 2013 Robert Vasvary

illustrations by Charlie Read

edited by Karen Gelhaar

Literary Agent and Legal Counsel

Jonathan Hibbert

ISBN 9780991076505

Library of Congress Control Number: 2013919895

For my son, Ethan Daniel Vasvary

I grew up in the Appalachian Mountains. As a kid, I remember rummaging through the "Big House." That is what my mother's family called it. Built in the early 1900's, it was a colossal two-story red brick structure with an absolute command of Main Street. Filled with relics, artifacts and history from that era, it brought another world into my senses. Every visit brought something new and undiscovered, like buried treasure. There was never enough time to see it all. Super high ceilings loomed upward carrying ornate carvings of cherubs and ladies' faces. Were they angels or demons watching me? They left me simultaneously unnerved and excited. At the end of every visit I could only dream of my next.

On one trip I found an antique silver saxophone. Through the tarnish and age, it shone directly into my soul. These days of discovery created in me a love of the unexpected and the extraordinary. The Big House is a story about self-discovery, imagination and never letting go of hope. Since my first visit, the Big House has never left me, frequently occupying my dreams even today.

Now a father, I wonder what my son's 'Big House' will be when he begins his age of discovery. Trust yourself is my advice. Intuition is the compass of your soul. Ethan, be true to your beliefs. Allow yourself to become who you really are. You have only one soul. Let it guide you. And even on the darkest days, if you remain true to yourself, you will always be filled with hope.

Everything is pitch black.
The tunnel walls feel soft and slimy.
A chill runs down his spine,
rising panic stuck in his throat.
The walls are breathing.

Plunged into a world where the
boundaries between fantasy and reality
have disappeared, Andy's thirst for
adventure leads him to precious treasure,
true love and unspeakable horror.
In a bid to escape the terrifying realm
of the undead and find the truth,
there is only one way out: an epic
showdown between good and evil
that challenges everything he knows
about himself and the world.

The Big House

Book One
Worlds Within

The Discovery

I will never forget the day my grandfather gave me my first tour of The Big House. The old house on Main Street was scary looking and rumors had it haunted. Two stories, red brick and built in the colonial style of the time, it had old weathered shutters, big windows and a rooftop balcony my grandfather, Papa Joe, called the "crow's nest." Local lore was that every now and then you could see the ghost of a little girl walking around up there. It had a dilapidated porch with big, round, rotting pillars. The woodwork had long since deteriorated.

My grandparents did not live in the house and preferred their small cottage next door. I was mildly curious about the house when I was doing yard work for them. Raking that huge lawn was my labor of love and of course, good pocket change. On the days when Papa Joe would be mowing the lawn, I would come down and start raking where he had just finished. He would be riding on the old farm tractor with huge rear tires, taking his time, smoking his cigarette and really enjoying his chores. For the longest time, I thought the house looked like any other old house on Main Street. I was only interested in yard money, finishing the job and rewarding myself with an ice cold RC Cola and a Moon Pie afterward.

But the more I worked around the grounds letting my mind wander, the more my curiosity grew and my imagination started to run wild when thinking about the rumors of the ghost.

I studied the old bricks, the window seals with the rotting trim and the smells that emanated from the basement. It was a sweet musty smell that I could only describe as the color purple. I even started making up stories of ghosts and goblins, adding to the town's tall tales of the girl ghost to the point that I would spook myself. Sometimes, while I was raking leaves, I had the feeling someone inside was watching me. Was it my imagination or was someone trying to get my attention? It was a fascinating stalemate. I was depriving myself of the experience of a lifetime.

Finally, I got the nerve to ask Papa Joe to show me the house. He just winked at me and said, "Sure Andy, I thought you would never ask."

That summer afternoon Papa Joe shared his old home with me. The heavy door creaked on rusty hinges, the sound flooding the house. I instantly felt chilled. Papa Joe grabbed my hand and smiled reassuringly. In the main foyer, our footsteps echoed as we crossed the wooden floor. It was like an empty gymnasium. I never suspected the vastness and instantly felt small.

There was no electricity. He quickly ushered me into the main foyer and out of the shadows. In the main hall the sun sprayed through the giant windows. Light danced as it bounced off the huge chandelier. The light show warmed the immense old room. Dust rose through the beams of light, looking like ghosts dancing around us.

Down the hall we came upon huge sliding doors. Papa Joe directed me to the living room. It was vast. Yellowing sheets covered the furniture. As we passed, a sheet fluttered in the commotion and brushed my hand. I jumped. Was it reaching for me?

Papa Joe put his hand on my shoulder and moved me on. The dining room was commanded by a long table. It was easy to imagine the King and Queen dining with their court. I could see the beast, with the steely knife at the ready. Another chill ran down my spine. It was dark again. Paintings of long gone family members hung in the dim light, eyes peering directly at me as I passed.

Pushing back my fear, I slid closer to my grandfather's side. Under close supervision he guided me from room to room, spilling bits of trivia about Big House family life. I was at first intimidated by the mysterious old house, but relished the excitement as any teenager would. I relaxed a bit, comfortable enough in his proximity to be able to marvel at the time gone by.

My attention to detail was on full. Rooms and relics transported me to a different time at any given moment, only to be snapped back by the sights and smells of the rambling old house. I was overwhelmed by the sheer volume of everything there was to explore. Every corner, every shadow had something new to be discovered. Secrets waiting to be shared and stories dying to be told called out from behind the crumbling old books, cobwebs and faded walls.

I was lost in the details. I saw fingerprint stains on dusty ancient lamps. Who did they belong to? When were they left? Were the piles of magazines exactly as they were when last read years ago? Was that pile of ash in the turn of the century tray a remnant of a guest from the last party, generations ago? Was anyone from that party still alive? Was that moment waiting to be rediscovered?

After that first day when I stepped through the front door with Papa Joe and got my first impression of The Big House, each new visit revealed more details I had not seen before. That was what boys my age thrived upon: adventure! I had no idea of the adventure on which I was about to embark.

Obsession

Weeks had passed since my first visit inside the Big House. Steve and I were sitting on the huge boulder that overlooked "The Fort" as I told him more of my visits. Steve was a friend I had made last summer while riding motorcycles on the old dirt roads that ran through the strip mine behind my neighborhood. Most times Steve and I would hang out there talking about stuff like our next construction phase or how to have some fun that day. Nestled in the woods over the hill from our lookout point, "The Fort" consisted of eight huge logs at least ten feet long, notched and overlapping in a perfect square. We had worked hard with axes to fall the trees and they had to be just right, so we cut only the best and biggest ones. It was only waist high to date and had no door. That was the next phase. No one had discovered the place yet as far as we knew, not even the Hopkins boys, the local thugs that lived in the trailer park down from my house. Our world there was a vast stretch of wilderness far removed from civilization even though the road to our school was just down the hill about a quarter of a mile through the woods. Plans for our future grand cabin took up a lot of our time. The boulder was our regular outpost at the edge of the woods that bordered the road where we kept alert for intruders.

But recently our conversation was focused on the Big House. Steve's interest had grown substantially since I started sharing my discoveries of the old place. You could tell by his expression that he was feeling the same fascination I had experienced and was getting anxious to see it. The only problem was that my mother didn't approve of my friend as he lived in the same trailer court as the Hopkins boys. She just assumed Steve was the same trailer court trash. I knew better. He was one cool dude with a big heart despite his rough exterior.

"Ever since Papa Joe gave me the tour, I have been consumed by the house. I even dream of the girl at night, the visions starting out in fantasy but always ending in nightmares," I told Steve. "Every time I go there I see something new that I never saw before. It's as if the house is revealing its secrets to me. It is funny how everything looks just like any old house, but once you zoom in and notice the details, the more it changes and the details stand up and present themselves. I think someone or something keeps moving things around so I see it the next time I come. It is almost as if the house recognizes my desire to discover more each time and is anticipating my return. But I get the feeling there are some things it is hiding so as not to scare me away. I think it has a dark side as well."

"You talk about it as if it was a person. Are you getting chicken?" he joked. "So when are you going to take me along, Andy? I can't wait any longer," Steve said impatiently.

"Soon," I replied. "I promise."

Treasure Hunting

After my first guided tour with Papa Joe, I had shown such genuine interest in the house that he told me where the spare key was hidden. I now had the key to a whole new world and an infinite opportunity to explore. I had made several visits to the house alone, each time getting more confident and less intimidated. My desire to explore was at its peak. There were old boxes and things piled up seemingly at random. That was the exciting part. The random placement of each and every thing showed order to me. I could see the history piled up in chronological order. The items on top of the piles within reach were the things most recently used and when I started digging into the past I could not stop. The deeper I dug, the more I was traveling back in time.

Despite clouds of dust kicked up from diving into the piles of junk (one man's junk is another man's treasure), I felt cleansed and alive by the thrill of the hunt. My mother would not say a word about my pigpen look when I would run in describing the day's treasure hunt through what she saw as "Papa Joe's junk." She would always advise jokingly, as mothers do, "Please be careful in there, babes. You never know what you may find."

One day she told me, "If you see a ghost, say hi for me! I am sure it would remember me from the days when I lived there as a kid. It may even become your friend knowing that you are my son!" We laughed together at this little joke but there was something about her statement that gave me the chills. Was she trying to spook me? What if it was real? I dismissed it as her way of helping me make light of the town's ghost stories.

It is true the place looked like a junkyard. My grandfather was a pack rat, but he was my hero from the moment I stepped into the house. He was a pioneer of sorts, who had the luxury of being raised in a time and place where his family had wealth, culture and exposure to the finer things. He was a mining engineer and had quite the grand reputation in that small Virginia coal-mining town and surrounding counties. In this town he might as well have been the mayor.

After all, his father, Napoleon Powell was one of the founding fathers of the town. It is rumored that the bricks for the old house were specially made by a British company his father had hired to build the house. He had the resources, knowledge and the ability to do whatever he desired. Back then, there was little time to be lazy. The Industrial Age was well underway and there was still much to create and invent. Everything I chanced upon was a time-stamp of progress of the United States of America. It was my own private Smithsonian! I found a ton of miscellaneous crap like pins that said "Truman for President," yardsticks from hardware stores in the roaring twenties, lighters, canes and my favorite; his medals from World War II.

I uncovered so many nostalgic items it felt as if I had traveled back in time and I could walk out the front door of the Big House to find Old Packards and model-T Fords, if not horse-drawn wagons, driving down the dirt road called Main Street.

The buttons, the pocket knives, Zippos (he loved them), the pipes, ashtrays and anything you could possibly find at a flea market filled every corner of the house — all piled up in the grand order of time when they were placed there. Aah the history! It was incredible.

Papa Joe was much more than a mining engineer. He was a literary connoisseur, a politician, an artist, a surveyor, an architect, a land owner and even an auctioneer. He was indeed the captain of his own vessel. Or was he just a nostalgia buff and a jack of all trades? I dared not label him. I wasn't that close to him, conversationally, at this age. I was merely his grandson and an admirer of his stuff. His world, all encased by a big old house, was my museum, and now part of my world to explore. It had my full attention and was luring me in.

As I sifted through what most would call refuse, I was as close as I could ever come to history. A history book could paint pictures in time but here, the sense of touch, sight and smell taught me lessons that books never would.

I had covered almost every room and had almost overturned everything in the house when I found a special room on the second floor. The doors must have been at least 20 feet tall, made of solid wood and very heavy.

The construction of this house was unparalleled, especially compared to the ones built today. The woodwork of the doors alone was unbelievable. "Was it walnut, oak or cherry?" I asked myself. They weren't on hinges but were the type that slid into the walls. They would slide open only a few inches and there were no door knobs, only a keyhole in the middle of brass plates. I could not squeeze through. They must have been rusted or off track. I slid my fingers into the opening and pulled with all my might, groaning and straining. The doors would not budge. I was determined to get in there. I tugged again and again until I had broken a sweat and exhausted my arms. Huffing and puffing, I leaned forward propping my arms on my knees, trying to catch my breath before my next attempt. I rested for a moment as the sweat rolled off my brow, when I heard something heavy shift from the other side and scatter across the room. I inserted my fingers in the crack and gave a hard tug. The doors squeaked and gave way, but only about a foot and I almost lost my balance falling forward through the crack, scraping my shoulders.

I stuck my head in to peer at the contents. Boxes were piled higher than I was tall. From what I could see, there were narrow passageways between the stacks of boxes that were like crooked, flimsy towers ready to fall at any moment. There were devices and treasures that, upon first inspection, I had no idea what they were. Jackpot! I had to get in there and I was not leaving until I did.

These were my grandfather's treasures, his most precious keepsakes. I was like a pirate who had stumbled onto the booty.

Some of the boxes had fallen forward, leaning against the doors. I was now challenged to move them to get in. I needed to push them away from the doors and I knew it was not going to be easy. I tried reaching through but I only had maybe a foot to squeeze in and my arms weren't long enough. The box on the right door would not budge and was just out of reach. I kept stretching my arms, my fingers barely making contact, until my body ached.

I leaned my belly into the crack, taking a breather and gazed into the room with pure excitement and wanderlust. How was I going to get that box off the door? I tried again but was soon exhausted and had to take another break. I would not give up and decided I would stay there all night if I had to.

I stood in front of the huge doors helpless and out of options. Frustration consumed me as I cursed my pathetic skinny body and kicked the door. As if the house extended a sympathetic hand, the boxes shuffled again and a thick old wooden cane fell between the gap in the doors presenting me the tool I needed to wedge that heavy box off the door long enough to slide it open. I pulled the sturdy cane up and slid it between the door and the box. My arms were stretched as far as they could and by then I knew I would have bruises on my armpits from leaning with all of my weight against the opening. I gave it a try but the box pushed away from me along the door, sliding further to the right.

"Dammit! This has to work," I commanded. I tried again but my strength was almost gone. I leaned up against the door trying to rest as long as my impatience would allow. I repositioned the stick and groaned loudly like a weightlifter that was going for a new record. The box gave way and tipped onto the floor away from the door. The right door slid open so quickly I fell forward into the room as more boxes and items fell towards me. I was buried alive but was in the room! I lay laughing in anguish and disbelief like the first-time gold medal winner who had victoriously pushed himself farther than ever before. I did not want to move for a moment and hadn't the strength or desire. I had won the fight! I lay there for what seemed like ten minutes and then pushed the lottery of treasures off me. I started putting things in order so I could at least move around the filled room. There was no hurry. Time did not exist, only precious exploration.

Realizing it was getting dark and I would be late for dinner, I started working faster. I wanted to see it all right now and I didn't want to leave. That is when I stumbled onto the case. It was a black case and even from the outside, an old musty smell emanated from it. It was at the bottom of a large stack of boxes and I had to summon my last ounce of strength to get to it. I pulled it up and propped it on top of other boxes. It had a brass plate with the word Selmer on it. When I opened it, I was mesmerized. It was a dingy old silver-plated Saxophone nestled in a bright blue velvet lining.

I gazed at my new-found treasure for what seemed like an hour. I was so entranced with it that I didn't realize the time. I only pulled my eyes from it when I noticed that there was little light in the room. It was dusk and I was getting cold even in August. The furnaces had not worked in years and the electricity was not on. I didn't even care that I was shivering but the realization that it was getting dark and I was still alone in the house suddenly gave me the creeps. No matter how excited I was with my new discovery, being in an old supposedly haunted house in the dark triggered panic that ran through my whole body. More importantly, I did not want to get in trouble and lose my privileges. I had to get home as I was now late for dinner. I was told I could not take anything from the house so I closed the case and put some boxes over it to conceal it.

Suddenly, I heard a shriek and the floor shook. Then I heard what sounded like the chandeliers clanging. This time I didn't freeze. I ran out of the room, down the stairs not daring to look around and out the front door making sure I quickly locked it behind me. Once outside, I kept running not sure if it was out of fear or thrill. I was no longer exhausted. My adrenaline was flowing as I ran up the street as fast as I could, past the six houses to get to our house on the hill. By the time I got home I had forgotten all about my scare. I could not wait to share the news of my treasure with my family. That was the first moment in my life where I felt I had a pirate's tale to tell.

The Chase

I will never forget the day that I met Steve. I was riding by myself around the track when the oldest of the unruly Hopkins boys, Eugene, jumped out from the bushes and stuck out his huge stump of an arm, knocking me off my bike. I fell backwards down the steep hill that bordered the second level facing the trailer court — sliding then rolling, crashing into rocks before landing in the bushes. Steve was riding his green machine that day and saw the whole thing go down.

After seeing my agonizing fall, Eugene smiled at his handiwork and yelled down the hill, "Take your pansy ass back home and lick your wounds you freakin' baby. And don't come back. This is our turf!" He turned and started back towards the trailer court to brag to his brothers. I just laid there for a moment, dazed and wondering which direction my bike went.

I stood up, rubbing my wounds, when I heard the roar of another motorbike, the rider, heading toward Eugene, who was strutting down the long path that led back to the trailer park where he lived. The driver revved up the KX in defiance, the engine screaming furiously. One strike of the driver's arm across Eugene's shoulders sent him flying into a deep gully off to the right.

My fall was bad, but I had rolled and blocked the obstacles with my arms. Eugene wasn't so lucky. He went face down into the gully, his face and chest digging into the gravelly soil before skidding to a stop ten feet later.

"Pick on someone your own size, punk!" the other boy shouted and gunned his bike in a final act of vengeance. Eugene stood up in the gully dumbstruck, holding his bloody face. His shirt was torn off and he had the worst case of road rash I had ever seen, all the way down his chest. Eugene was stockier than the other boy, and a bit taller. Eugene was normally intimidating with his crude demeanor, oily black hair and muscle shirts. But now he looked like a pathetic shrimp standing down in the gutter with Steve looming over him. He looked like he wanted to cry as he wiped the dirt and gravel off his face and I struggled to stifle the urge to laugh. I just stood there relishing the moment, forgetting all about my wounds. This kid had come to my rescue. The two younger Hopkins brothers, hearing the skirmish, were running up the hill from the trailer court to Eugene and tried to help him out of the rut. He pushed them away in embarrassment. For such a bully he looked harmless as he crawled out of the ditch, angrily dusting himself off.

"What the hell did you do that for, Steve?" screamed Bobby, the taller and lankier of Eugene's two younger brothers.

"He clothes-lined that kid for no reason at all. He could have broken his neck," Steve said with ferocity in his voice.

"He was minding his own business riding his bike. That was bullshit and uncalled for. This isn't your track."

"If I catch y'all picking on him or anyone else, I will do much worse the next time. Now get the hell out of here before I get off this bike and kick all y'alls asses," Steve warned.

I watched as the three brothers scurried down the hill mumbling obscenities. Steve revved his bike again, spun around, popped a wheelie and raced back up the hill to where I was assessing my bike and myself for damages.

"Are you OK?" he asked. Concern registered in his voice but his face showed no sympathy. Steve was bigger and older than I was and I should have been intimidated, but after defending me, I knew he was a good guy and I was grateful.

"Yeah, I'll be alright," I replied, still shaken up. "I usually don't come down here if I know those jerks are around. I didn't see anyone when I got here. He must have heard me riding and snuck up on me. Thanks for sticking up for me."

Steve got off his bike and walked over to mine, checking it over. I could smell gasoline. He helped me pull it out of the bushes and back onto the path, propping it on the kickstand. The gas tank was badly dented and leaking.

"I think your gas tank has a hole in it. That sucks. It ain't gonna be cheap to replace. I guess you better push it home so you don't catch it on fire."

"Thanks again man." I paused, looking at the damaged bike, sighed then stuck out my hand. "My name is Andy. What's yours?"

"I'm Steve." He hesitated then shook my hand without

making eye contact. He continued, "I live in the first trailer on the right as you come in the park. Them Hopkins boys are scum. They make everyone here miserable. I wish they would move."

"Yeah, me too," I agreed. "This track is fun and I will keep coming here but I guess I will have to watch my back more closely."

"Just stay away from them. They are real trouble and love to fight. You'll have to stand up to them sooner or later or they'll keep picking on you. They did the same to me until I kicked Eugene's ass two days after I moved here."

"Hey, I have a secret fort I'm working on," I offered.

I pointed down the long dirt road that led to the Grand Woods. Do you want to go riding one day and I'll show it to you?"

"Cool," Steve said as hopped back on his bike. "I gotta' get going now. It's almost time for supper. Later." He cranked up his bike and rode off, the engine screaming so loud I cupped my hands over my ears.

I dusted myself off and started the long push home. My muscles and joints ached. And on top of that, when I arrived, mom took one look at me and had a fit. I told her I fell off the bike in fear that she would ground me from the track if she knew I had a run-in with punks from the trailer court.

The track was the remains of an old strip mine behind the trailer court and my neighborhood that butted up to many acres of forest. It had never been reclaimed properly. It had been carved out over the years by the kids with motorcycles who lived nearby to form a motocross. It was the ultimate playground. It had ramps, roundabouts and huge hills we would challenge each other to climb. It had two levels. The lower level had a fairly perfect circle and a horseshoe against the embankment of the upper level where we could do endless laps relatively fast. Instead of continuing around the horseshoe on the first level we could stay straight and go to the second level, which was about a ten foot "jump up." Once on the second level we had to be more careful as it had many natural obstacles like rocks, trees, bumps and mud puddles which made it that much more exciting and challenging. This track was dirt bike heaven. Behind it ran miles of old strip mine scars that set the stage for incredible adventures.

This was life in the wilderness of rural Virginia with beautiful trails, vines to swing on, forts to build, caves to explore and huge rock formations to climb. When the woods lost our interest, we'd hang out behind Kennedy's store, in an alley hidden from the main flow of shoppers, where we were unlikely to be spotted.

My father had bought me a bright orange Kawasaki KD125. It wasn't a little kid's bike like my first mini-bike, a little Indian 50. My mom was against me having a bike at all but Dad reassured her I was ready. It was the best gift my father ever gave me. Of course everything comes with a price, and ever since then, I had become the resident landscaper of the household as payment for the "gift."

My Kawasaki had much more power than the old mini-bike and I thought it was fast until I saw Steve's bike, a bright green Kawasaki KX175. I was really proud of my mountain bike, but it was no match for Steve's "Green Machine" which was made for motorcross racing. His had a power band and it would scream like a scalded wildcat on the long open stretches of trails. Mine didn't have a power band but it was equipped with a huge rear sprocket. I could climb the steepest hills with ease. Steve's bike would usually stall out on the steep and winding trails and he couldn't keep up with me. On the track we were a close race but on the straightaways, he would leave me in his dust. In the hills and trails he was no match for me and he hated it.

I went to the track often. I made sure the coast was clear, when Steve was not around, for fear of getting beat up by the Hopkins boys. If they were there I would avoid the track and continue racing down the mining road that led to the Grand Woods; that is what we called the miles of undeveloped land between the track and the road by the high school. I would just keep on going and pretend I never saw them.

One day, this time on foot, Steve and I met a ways down the old mining road that connected my dead-end street to the track. We met here so my mother would not know I was associating with people from the trailer park, something I knew she would disapprove of.

I had told Steve all about my discoveries in The Big House, and this was the day I was to show him inside. Unfortunately, the Hopkins Boys had seen us and we realized they were headed our way. I imagine they had overheard us talking about the grand old house and it had piqued their curiosity. Now the Hopkins boys were hot to see the inside of the house, too. Steve had told them it would never happen after how they'd treated me. Recently, Eugene had been spotted peering into windows on the front porch of the Big House. Someone had called the cops and Eugene thought that someone was me!

We took off down the mining road before veering off the path and ducking into the brush, hoping to throw them off.

"I can't wait to show you the old house, Steve!" I exclaimed, trying to catch my breath. "Wait until you see what treasures I've uncovered. It is awesome! I don't want to tell you now. I want it to be a surprise." After a while, convinced we had outrun them or they'd dropped the pursuit, we started back down the mining road, slowing our pace to a jog.

"Don't worry about them, Andy. They're just jealous" Steve said, adding, "I've heard them talking about trying to sneak in since they found out it was your grandfather's house."

I answered, "I would take them if it would bring some peace between us."

"Forget them!" Steve demanded. "They would just take advantage of you. They don't respect anyone or anything, much less themselves. They would probably come back, break in and trash the place later like they did at Mr. O'Deele's workshop. Don't try to get on their good side. They don't have a good side. It's just not worth it."

The Hopkins boys were nothing but punks. It was rumored that that their father dealt drugs and beat his wife. They were always trying to pick a fight with me, or throwing threats around. I was not the only one they targeted, though. The police were regular visitors at their trailer. They were in constant trouble with the law and always wanted someone to be their punching bag. They were a scruffy bunch and easily identified as scoundrels by the way they skulked around town, dressed in ratty old clothes and cussed with every sentence.

I had to admit they had a special hatred for me. They knew that I was Steve's friend and they just could not understand why he would hang out with a kid outside their turf. It wasn't my fault that I lived in the adjoining neighborhood in a decent house and Steve knew that I wasn't a rich spoiled kid, but an average boy. Steve was always protecting and defending me and every now and then, like when we met, we'd get the upper hand on them.

In a short time, Steve and I had become riding buddies and great friends even though we tried to keep it from our family and peers. It was a burden for him at times because he was constantly defending me. He always had my back even when he was heckled for being my friend. Steve and I were stuck in different social classes and although he was big and brawny, he was kind-hearted. I could see it in his eyes, but the Hopkins boys didn't get him. They were too busy selfishly looking inward. Steve hid his good nature when around them and projected a rough exterior to fit the trailer court set. He had an unconditional respect for all that is good in this world but kept it hidden from those who did not have the same capacity. His father had taught him well to feel for others.

"There are bad apples in every bunch and they are rotten," he would say of the Hopkins Boys. "We can smash them and make apple wine to keep us happy." Even though he appeared to be a bully, he amazed me every time he would make comments like this (only around me and his petite girlfriend, Heather). It was difficult to imagine those words coming from such a tough guy. I am glad that Steve had a tender side. He was a diamond in the rough and on his bike he was like a super hero.

I never showed my face in the trailer court without being in his presence. I knew that none of the Hopkins boys would stand up to him one on one. As a group however, they were like a fierce pack of wolves preying on anyone they thought they could overtake. Yet, they normally hesitated to mess with Steve even in a group. He had a volatility they could sense. They dared not push his limits. But, on this hot August day, they crossed the line.

"Steve," I said, "When we get to my street, wait there for me. I will tell my Mom I am walking to town. That will buy us plenty of time to go visit the house, too. Stay low. Don't let her see you or I won't get to go."

"Sure buddy," he said, still out of wind.

"I hate that your parents don't like me. I am not like those assholes," he complained.

"I know. It's not fair," I said. "I hate being judged too. That's OK. We will always be friends, man. They'll come around some day," I reassured him. We were getting the same pressure from both sides when we hung out so we had to keep a low profile. In small towns, people loved to gossip and label you. Sneaking around to protect our bond had become a condition of our friendship. At school we didn't hang out together. Today, Steve wanted to see inside the mysterious Big House and I couldn't wait to show it to him.

From the forest, we heard leaves rustling and sticks breaking, and realized the Hopkins Boys were still in pursuit. "I'm sorry I got you into this Steve", I said, the sweat dripping down my face. My heart was pounding and panic rushed into my veins like an arctic blast.

"One day they will get theirs, Andy."

"I just hope I am around to see it," he said with a grimace. We ran with all our strength and they fell out of sight again.

We left the dirt road, crossing through the small patch of thick bushes and met the pavement at the dead end of my street where he was to wait for me. We slowed our pace, trying to catch our breath. We had planned on taking the mining road to the cut-through at the cemetery that met the back yard of The Big House, avoiding my house, my grandparents, and being seen together on Main Street.

As I was about to head towards my house to get permission to go to town, I heard their voices and turned to see that they were holding rocks, aiming them at us and ready to strike. Steve and I didn't hesitate and started running just as one zipped by my head, barely missing me and creating dust as it landing in dirt. Now they were after us for real. They wanted blood. Today they would punish us both for Steve protecting me on their turf. Steve was right. They were jealous. But it was more than that.

Just as we came out of the cut-through from the dirt road at the end of my street and hit the pavement, two of the three boys cut us off. We tried to skirt around but Eugene ran up from behind us where he had been hiding in the bushes and grabbed my shirt.

"Traitor," growled Eugene, as he turned to Steve and wiped the snot onto his shirt sleeve from his sweaty face. His face was steaming and red as if his head was about to explode.

"Where do you think you're going?" They all were holding rocks in their hands and crammed in their pockets. They were ready for battle.

"Come on man, let Andy go." Steve demanded. He shoved Eugene, breaking his grasp on my shirt and I landed on the pavement with my knee taking the blow.

"Asshole" I muttered in pain. "Leave us alone and maybe you can go next time," I said, although I knew there was no way in hell they would ever get that chance. Steve grabbed Eugene's two brothers, and yelled, "Run Andy, now!" I wasted no time getting to my feet and hitting a full sprint.

Steve shoved the two boys into Eugene, they fell in a heap to the pavement and he took off behind me. We regained speed but they quickly caught up and were right behind us. We could hear threats and profanity getting closer. They were furious and I was scared. I could see that Steve was scared. He never showed fear but this time we had really pissed them off. They were out for blood. I could see my house and the pine trees that lined the yard just ahead. Once we made it past the pines we would be safe. We were only 80 feet away and Steve ran in the other direction from my house to divert them.

"Home free," I thought prematurely.

They were gaining on me, but I didn't look back. That is when I felt a sharp pain above my right kidney and another in the middle of my back.

The pain was so sharp I almost lost my balance but dared not stop and managed to stay on my feet and keep running. "Dammit!" I half screamed and half pleaded, "You'll get yours, I swear it. Cut it out!" Only 40 feet to go now. I cut through a neighbor's yard and barreled toward my backyard. I could see my house and my mom was sweeping the back porch. Then I heard a loud thump and felt a bolt of electricity from the back of my head followed by a ringing sound so loud I thought it was a train…

The Descent

I was standing in front of the Big House. The high-pitched screech like that of a train on a collision course echoed in my ears and made my head ache terribly, but the sound was slowly fading. The sun shined so bright in my face, at first I was not sure it was the same house. "How did I get here? What day is it? What is going on? Where is Steve? Did I get permission to go to my grandparents and if so why isn't Steve here with me?" I asked myself all these questions at once not even able to attempt an answer. Before I could get my sense of orientation, the dark shadows of the front porch started moving.

Usually the front entrance to the place was a bit unnerving. A westerly view and two huge trees cast a perpetual shadow that no sun ever penetrated, the heavy shade giving the house a deserted air. The porch was really large and extended to the left beyond the steps back around to the street and opened in a small semicircle, like a pavilion. With what white paint remained, bare wood exposed and weathered, the porch looked in danger of imminent collapse. Slats were missing here and there and the ones remaining were rickety. The windows had not been cleaned in years.

Cobwebs added to the look of a haunted house. Several broken rocking chairs had retired in the pavilion and were rotting along with the surface boards, becoming one with the decking.

But today, the big old house looked like new!

The sun had stretched onto the porch and beams of light splayed across the boards. The rocking chairs now looked relatively new and without much sign of faded white paint. The surface of the deck was clean and the windows gleamed in the sun. "Ok, what is going on here?" I asked myself out loud.

Maybe my interest in the place made my grandparents realize it was time to fix the place up and they hired someone to clean up the porch. The entrance looked almost immaculate. "This looks like a month's worth of work at least."

Before I could question this peculiar scene any further, I noticed the front door was wide open. I went into panic mode.

No way! Papa Joe would kill me! I would never hear the end of it and I would be denied access which means my adventures would be over. Then I thought about the saxophone. Fear surged through my body, a chill went down my spine and then it felt like a thousand volts pushing my nervous system into overload. For a moment I just stood there, paralyzed. My head started spinning and my vision went blurry.

Suddenly, the house started growing! It was coming to life in front of my eyes. It was stretching up and around, looking like it was growing a third story, while the porch followed the new angles as the house added more dimensions and windows until it looked like the most beautiful hotel I had ever seen.

As the house continued to grow, it was moving farther away from me as if the ground was rising, sending it up a hill. I rubbed my eyes trying to shake off my delusions but to no avail. It looked even more real and in focus. I hoped that it was all in my head and tried to concentrate on the saxophone. Without hesitation, I ran up the porch stairs, fully expecting the first step not to be there. My foot made contact with the steps and I felt an instant of fear but ignored it, thinking only of checking on my precious bounty. As I traversed the stairs I felt as if I was floating, being propelled upward to the front door. I was electrified and petrified all at once, but was not deterred. I pushed through the entrance, making a beeline to the room on the second floor.

I passed through the main foyer and headed straight for the stairs. Out of the corner of my eye, the foyer appeared the size of a cathedral. Hoping that it was just my mind playing tricks on me, I dared not let it distract me from my mission and kept running to the stairs, which by now was a colossal version of the stairs I knew. I heard the front door slam shut behind me and felt another wave of disorientation. I did my best to ignore it and lunged forward, taking the steps two at a time. The stairwell seemed much longer than I recalled. The more I tried to focus on climbing, the farther away the second floor appeared. Now it felt like I wasn't moving.

"This isn't right. This isn't right," I kept repeating in my head. The blood was pumping through my legs so fast they hurt and my heart felt like it was going explode. I was going nowhere! What was going on?

From behind me I heard scampering like that of claws on a slippery floor followed by a deafening howl, then others. It sounded like a pack of mad wolves growling and snarling and they were coming for me!

I scrambled up the stairs refueled by pure terror not daring to look back. When I looked down I realized the stairs were gone, nothing but blackness below. Bolts of electricity coursed through my head again and the screeching in my ears was replaced by howls from the demon beasts, making me grasp my ears in pain. Then everything got extremely bright as if the sun had exploded and I could not see!

That was when I started falling; unaware of anything, except that I was in sensory overload. I was spinning out of control helplessly and falling faster and faster. As I was kicking my legs and waving my arms uncontrollably out of hysteria, I heard a voice whisper ever so softly, "You're going to be alright. I'm here. You will be OK."

Then the voice changed to a more morbid and commanding tone. "Just hang on and stay awake. I have some things I need to show you." Amidst all the chaos, I must have passed out, for the next thing I knew, I found myself motionless and in total darkness. At this point I was only aware that I was no longer falling and was lying on the ground and had no idea where I was.

I tried to get a grip on what just happened and tried to stop shaking and get control of myself. I felt like I was in a movie, flashing from scene to scene but unable to recall the previous one. For a moment, I had no recollection of falling or running up the stairs but my head and legs ached terribly. Where in the hell was I? It was pitch black, damp and cool. I could not see a thing, not even the hands in front of my face. I suddenly realized I was holding something that I could not, at first, recognize. I ran my hands up and down the object, surveying it with my palms. Then I remembered! It was the cane that I had used to wedge open the door to the room full of Papa Joe's valuables. It was made of strong wood but was light and easy to wield.

"How did I get the cane? Did I make it up the stairs?" My sense of time was no longer continuous. My thoughts were random and it was hard to stay focused on the place I was in now, where I had been and how I got here.

There were so many questions in my head, but for some reason I was not scared or confused. I did not feel lost, but protected and guided. "Why do I feel like I am supposed to be here? How did I get this cane? Am I about to embark on a journey? Who is my tour guide?" I recalled hearing a voice but let all those concerns go, for I needed to know where I was now. For some reason, though, I felt safe in knowing I would be taken care of and that I should just enjoy the ride. It was like having someone I trust putting a bandage over my eyes, holding my hand and leading me to the surprise.

I have always trusted all my senses equally. I was fortunate to have them intact and none were more superior to the others. My intuition gave me security in knowing that my senses would never mislead me. I learned this lesson early in life, reflecting for a moment when my mother prepared liver for the first time. My gut feeling told me not to try it. I poked it with my knife first. It was firm, like meat, but with a rubbery texture, sorta like the surface I was standing on now. It smelled pungent. Strike two! It looked dark, almost black. That couldn't be good. And it tasted like YUCK! It had a pasty texture and was very rich and I could not wash the flavor from my mouth, even after a glass of milk. "Never again," I said to myself. I should have trusted my first impression before putting this foul substance in my mouth. "I do not like liver" will be my answer to this day. My senses knew that and I should have listened. My senses nor my intuition were of any help here. I again tried to make out my surroundings; so much for having the sense of sight. "So this is how it feels to be blind," I surmised.

I stretched out the cane and started poking around. Like sonar, the vibrations from striking objects should give me clues. As I jabbed my cane into the emptiness, I could not hear a sound, not even an echo from my breathing. There must be something protruding. I ran the course of my circumference and all around me was nothing. Above me was nothing.

I tapped the cane beside my feet and it felt gelatinous, like mud. It was soft and damp, like earth but I could not penetrate it.

It had elasticity and memory, but not like a trampoline. It was a bit more firm, almost alive, fleshy. Every time I pushed downward with the cane, the floor would give, like pushing a finger in your belly and would expand back to its original position. Was I standing on rubber of some kind? I slowly bent over, leaning on the cane and ran my hand over the surface below me. It was like touching a slimy fish.

The next idea I pondered was quite unsettling. I could be inside the belly of an animal. That is silly! How would I know what that would feel like? The next thought was even more absurd: Is it like being in my mother's womb? Thinking I could actually recall those pre-birth moments made me almost giggle and then terror overtook me at the thought that I had been consumed by some huge beast. My sense of touch had hit overload by now and I investigated it no more, feeling safe in the fact that I was at least standing on somewhat solid ground.

My nose took the lead now in the investigation as I immediately recalled the smell in this place. The only way I could describe it was that it smelled like the color purple. "Where had I smelled that odor?" It was like I had just discovered it again for the first time. This feeling of aromatic déjà vu irritated me as I could not recall where I had met this stench, but I knew I had recently encountered it elsewhere. It was sweet, like candy. In my mind, the word "opium" bubbled to the surface. "That is ridiculous. First of all, I am 13 and have never tried drugs." I had no clue what it was, where it came from or how it smelled except from the Wizard of Oz where I remember someone saying that it came from poppy flowers like when Dorothy and the gang fell asleep when they were running through the field to see the wizard. My nose was positive of this for some reason.

Was I recalling this scent from someone else's experiences, drawing from their recollection? Again, something told me that I wasn't alone. A chill ran through me and all of a sudden I was petrified. "Who was there with me, watching me, leading me through this, impressing their thoughts onto my mind? What did they want from me? Where was I going? I want my mother!" As soon as this thought was conceived, I was at ease again. It was almost as if she was right there with me holding my hand. My mom was my guiding light. Or was it an angel? Whoever was with me, I felt completely safe. My curiosity and sense of adventure were in charge again and I went straight back to my Sherlock Holmes mode assessing the facts. I was at the mercy of my senses but they had come up with no answers yet.

Now, I was all ears. At first all I perceived was dead silence. I waited, holding perfectly still, until I could only hear my heartbeat. The more I listened, the louder the sound became; per-thump, per-thump, Per-thump, Per-Thhump, Perrrrr-Thummmp, PERRRRR-THUMMMP.

Okay, I was just psyching myself out.

I tried to stay focused but I could not hear any other sound. I could have sworn I could even hear the blood rushing through my ears. Swish-whhoooo, swish-whhoooo. "Stop it!" I said out loud and then laughed nervously at my wild imagination. As my hearing adjusted, the sound of my own voice echoed in this place so loud, I was again alarmed. My slight chuckle resonated, but had direction. It had an echo. I was not in a closed area. There was a way out! I filled my lungs only a quarter of the way and said, "Hello."

The response was, "Hello, helllloo, hell-loooow, hell-loow, hell-loooow, helehlehelehello." It was a trick. It had no symmetry. No traceability. No direction. I tried again but still couldn't tell the proportions of the chamber I was in. I let out a sigh, and immediately following it, I heard laughter. I was not alone! Now, I felt surrounded and helpless, like the prey of some wild beast. "Remain calm," I repeated to myself like a mantra and that seemed to help. What was that? It sounded like a little girl. I held my breath, trying to ignore the thunderous sounds of my own body pumping blood through my veins. I waited but heard nothing.

I stood motionless, waiting to hear what I thought was a child's laughter, but again, nothing. I waited longer and it seemed like an eternity, every muscle in my body stiff like rigor mortis. I was so tense my right calf started to cramp. Being one who was born with a major deficit, lack of patience, I timidly whispered again, "hello," and it was immediately followed by the same laughter, like from a young girl.

"Hello," I said again and received the same reply. Once more I spoke these words, demandingly. The response was reciprocally louder as well. I reached out my walking stick in the direction of the laughter and put one foot forward. I was indeed experiencing the world from the perspective of a blind person, taking every step ever so carefully, not putting all my weight on the forward foot until sure, checking twice before shifting my weight and stepping again. I had taken three steps and my confidence was starting to grow. Each time I spoke a bit louder, the voice would respond and soon I found myself speaking and walking in the direction of the source, my pace quickening, but being careful not to slip. The more I spoke, the faster I went until I was in full stride, ignoring the pitch black, but trusting my ears. They told me that I had a ways to go.

I hadn't noticed that a faint glow had appeared in the distance. Light! I could see light at the end of the tunnel but the light was above me, indicating I was in a hole. I picked up the pace, focusing more on the light now and sparing my vocal cords, but not stopping in fear of losing communication with the girl's voice. At one point the voice seemed so close as if only feet away. Then I heard a different startling voice crying, "Come back" in a mother's stern commanding way. I stopped dead in my tracks, fear rising up in me.

"Hello," I said, one more time. No response.

Again I tried and received no feedback. I could definitely see the light now and it appeared that I was in a tunnel and it was starting to take an upward turn.
The light was bright enough that I could begin to see the walls.

They were brown, black, purple and blue and slightly reflective, as if a thin slimy coating adhered to them like an otter's pelt. There were roots starting to appear, like the leaves of a fern with very fine hairs covering them. I had endured enough and took off pulling on the roots and climbing upwards toward the light despite my fear of falling, concentrating only on the light ahead and getting out of this place.

Beating Murphy

I had been climbing for what seemed like hours, taking each step carefully to avoid slipping and having to start all over again. The light I was pursuing must have been bending but that was physically impossible. When it seemed that I was almost there, the excitement (somewhat like nearing the end of a rollercoaster ride) would wane. Just as I anticipated the end of this place, the tunnel would curve and the light would crawl to the other side of the wall in front of me revealing another bend in the tunnel. I was in 8th grade now and from what I had learned in science class, light could not bend like that. Maybe I was hallucinating from the fall. Had I fallen?

With my adrenal level at its current state, I was still in a state of dementia. When I tried to think back, a sharp pain would run through my head and straight down my spine. I was aware of my lack of short-term memory but had no control over it. Some powerful force kept me drawn to the here and now, not allowing me physically, mentally or emotionally to backtrack. It was like mind control and I felt vulnerable.

Now the light at the end of the tunnel was slowly but surely getting closer, but oddly enough the tunnel was twisting and turning like I was in the small intestines of some animal. The light would reflect off the left wall and then shift to the right. There were moments when I felt I was escalating upward in a circular motion like being on the entrance ramp to a parking garage.

I was running out of strength, my legs screaming for me to stop but that was not going to happen. I had to get out of there. The scent I had smelled since my arrival in this place seemed to make me feel better, having a euphoric property as well as a pain reliever. Maybe it was opium. Whatever it was, I was sure it was partially responsible for my super endurance as I had been running, crawling and climbing longer than humanly possible. I knew my limitations and had long surpassed them, but I had to press on. This place was creepy and hopeless.

Just like every time I began an afternoon project around the Big House raking leaves for my grandparents and earning spending money, I could not wait to finish. Sometimes my impatience got the best of me and I attempted to take a shortcut such as skipping an area that required raking. This always backfired. My grandmother Nini thoroughly inspected the jobsite before I got paid and would notice the infraction first thing, costing me another 30 minutes of work.

Ultimately, this helped instill a strong work ethic and taught me the value of persistence. My grandparents and my father reinforced these traits although attention to detail was my own gift from God. I was a perfectionist for a kid my age. As we walked around during inspection, I took great pride in the pristine lawn. The real reward was going straight down to Main Street after work to old man Kennedy's grocery and treating myself to an RC Cola in a cold longneck bottle and a

Moon Pie. I would sit on the old hand-carved stone wall that ran along the street, count the blisters on my fingers, my money and the cars as they passed by. My persistence and efforts were always rewarded by these moments.

Now, while battling to escape this place, my perseverance kicked in. Every time I wanted to stop, sit down or collapse from the never-ending climb, the light would grow in intensity ever so slightly and I would push on with renewed hope. I knew who was doing this to me now. I was sure of it. It was Murphy!

Papa Joe had once told me of 'Murphy's Law'. This law should be in the science books as well. Murphy's Law states that when you desperately want something to happen it will not happen. It avoids you until you are racked with disgust. Papa Joe explained that ONLY when you have given up and forgotten about what it is you so desperately wanted to happen, NOW, it shows up on your doorstep mockingly surrendering itself to you. It is the same when you have something on the tip of your tongue, like the name of an actor in a movie or a song you can't remember.

"The cat doesn't have your tongue. It is Murphy," he would always remind me. I hated Murphy and it always made me feel better to blame it on someone fictitious rather than real. He knew me, all too well. He used my impatience as a weapon against me. I was born without that chromosome. But I also knew that my best weapon against him was persistence.

I would have to fight him until he was again bored with me.

My father had agreed that we shared this lack of patience. Never mind that he told me I was also born lacking tact. Tact is, from what I was told, knowing how to speak, what to say AND knowing when not to speak. With my overactive imagination and gift of expression, it has always been a challenge to suppress the need to share my emotions.

Through the odd jobs I did at my grandparents, I learned I could never beat Murphy. Papa Joe would also say that once I was older, Murphy's Law would be a #1 rule with girls. The more you want them to like you, the more likely they would not. He advised, "The secret is to pretend you don't like them and they will come to you, thus beating Murphy at his own game." I was never good at that either. With my perfectionist mentality and drive, playing games to achieve my goals didn't make sense and seemed counterintuitive. So far I had not had many opportunities to exercise that phenomenon with girls. I was not quite interested in them yet. For now, they were just too fluffy and fragile for my likes. I wasn't ready to play that game. I just took Papa Joe's word on that.

This arduous climbing had gone on too long. I was about to stop for a moment just to challenge Murphy, despite my desire to finally be free of this place and I swear just the thought of it must have been heard by the man himself.

I rounded the last corner and came to a halt. The light was shining through the most beautiful stained-glass door that I had ever laid eyes on. It was on the same grand scale as the windows at our church, which were at least 20 feet tall and when the light shined through them, a million colors danced inside. I would always imagine angels playing in the colorful light as we sang hymns. The light coming through this glass released colors that seemed to swirl around the walls and on my shirt. The patterns reminded me of a pool where the ripples of water radiated outward in waves.

I just stood there for a moment catching my breath and marveling at the carousel of lights, wondering how long I had been down here, where I was and what kind of world I was in. Was it a door? There was no door knob. I looked all along the wall and could see no way out.

Below me, an old wooden board creaked. That couldn't be! I knew I was in a tunnel of sorts but indeed, when I looked down at my feet, I was suddenly standing on stairs. How did I not notice the transition from an earthly tunnel to stairs? I could see all around me now with the light glimmering from the stained glass. I turned and looked intently into the darkness behind me, trying to recall my furious struggle to make it here.

The tunnel was no longer there. All I could see was a long staircase plunging downward into darkness. Everything was in monotone: black, white and grey. There were no colors. I turned back to the door and held up my hand. The light on my hand was full of vivid colors dancing all along my arm. I turned again to the stairs and the same effect was rendered.

Nothing but black and white was displayed in my trail back down the tunnel. Maybe I had damaged my vision, I thought as the panic started to rise again realizing I was still trapped in this place. I immediately turned to the door, looking for any way to get out. I pushed and kicked the door in desperation. It would not budge. It made a deep echo when I banged on it with the cane, at least indicating there was something on the other side.

I began to beat my fists against the door screaming, "Help! Is there anyone out there? I am trapped. Down here." I listened for any signs of a presence on the other side but there was nothing but silence. I began to run my hands around the edges. The wood was solid, but rough and aged so I used caution not to get splinters. If there was no door knob how would I ever escape? My right hand moved over a metallic surface and I could not see what it was, but was sure it was a keyhole in the place where the door knob was or should have been. I put my eye up to the keyhole. The light was bright near the door, but after a moment I could see the definition of the hole. Beyond that was nothing but grey light and shadows. It was definitely the keyhole to the door but I could not tell where I was. After staring for a few moments, I could see a hallway, a long passage that disappeared into darkness. There was no furniture, so I could not see where I was in the house.

I was sure it was not the main hallway from the entrance or I would have seen the front door. I tried calling for help several times and was only rewarded by silence. My panic returned and I screamed at the top of my lungs, beating and clawing at the door. It was no use; I was lost here and was never going to be rescued. I was cold, scared and hopeless. I leaned against the door with one eye through the keyhole, sobbing and breathing hard. I tried to recall how I had gotten here. Sharp pain raced back up my spine and into my head like a hammer and I gave up trying to understand what was happening and why I was here. I just kept sobbing and focused as hard as I could on the keyhole hoping to see someone, anyone who could rescue me. Surely someone would be looking for me, I prayed. Time had become an unnecessary burden now as I had no idea how to measure it. I just stared at the keyhole.

"I wonder if I am even in the Big House at all," I thought, recalling faint images of a grandiose version of the house with the huge entrance.

I considered that I might be in the back of the house where I had not yet dared to venture, where the servants had once lived. Nothing looked familiar from this view. I just kept my eyes on the keyhole and the more I focused, the darker it seemed to get. The light from the stained glass was fading as well. Was night coming? I was unable to even think about how I got here, how long I was in the tunnel or even what day it was. My mind had endured more than it could handle but I would not remove my eyes from the keyhole.

I recalled the saxophone somewhere in the house and how it shined as if recognizing my admiration. The way the cold metal felt in my hands, made me feel like I had been armed with a mighty sword. This thought eased my exhausted mind and as I fantasized of playing that magical horn, I eased down to the stairway landing and drifted to sleep.

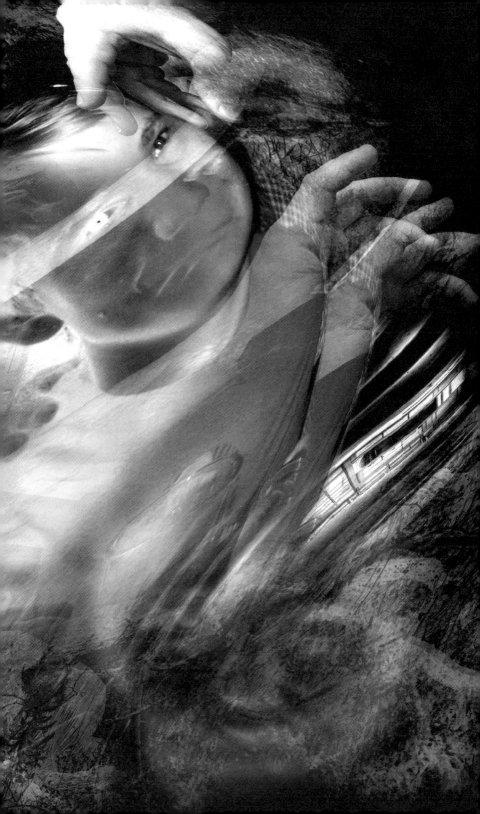

The Portal

I love the feeling of waking certain mornings to find the future ooh so bright. These are the best nights, when sleep brings visions of hope and you snap back into reality with a smile on your face, the belly of your soul content, survival being so far from your mind that you can't wait to face the day. If only we could be this carefree all our days as these moments, feeling revitalized and ever so joyful. Compared to waking from a nightmare where you want to go back to sleep, hide or just fight to shake off the negativity that you had escaped from, this was the way to go. Of course you can't really control how you will wake up.

Some days it is so hard to see the glass as half full. The forces of gravity, the celestial bodies and the environment play so much in controlling these emotions. The experiences and thoughts we go to bed with can fester while the subconscious works to purge the evil and despicable thoughts that slowly erode your soul. Each night that we take these ill feelings to bed, the mind goes to work to eradicate them. We carry them all our days if we cannot get them from our minds and the subconscious is slowly warped into a beast that has nothing but malice as it can find no resolution to its conscious dilemma. Resolve comes from enduring the pain and self-consuming fears that you took to bed with you either to be spit out by morning or carried into the next day like a heavy sack of unbearable weight.

It must have been the result of my accomplishing the arduous climb out of that horrid place to reach the door that had born me this optimistic reawakening. As I awoke, it took a moment to discern where I was now. I felt warmth and light on my face, embellished by the same brilliant colors that I had seen at the end of the tunnel. Except for the light shining down to again douse me in the full spectrum of colors, my position had changed. I was on the other side of the door and out of the tunnel! I was standing over a body sleeping spread out in front of the same stained glass door. With a shock, I suddenly realized that the person I was looking down upon was me! I could also see a girl leaning over me. I rubbed my eyes, trying to wake up from this dream but could not. She was watching me sleep, unmoving.

She was fair-skinned and slight with brown hair. She wore a white dress with a high collar and old-fashioned white patent leather shoes, like what I had seen in pictures from my grandmother's family albums. I had never seen her before. I was sure of that. Despite the angle of the light, I could see her face. Her features were clear and much in focus. Her eyes were smiling but her lips didn't reveal it. The rest of her face was pale and solemn. She looked very tired. She reached out her hand and touched my hair. When she did, it was like being hit by a bolt of lightning.

The lights from the stained glass door came alive and there was that same deafening scream. Now I was being propelled back down the tunnel and it felt as if I was being pulled by giant arms that sent pain through my head and down my spine. I was once again in sensory overload with all the noise.

Again, I awoke, breathing hard and fully alert but in shock. It is strange how dreams can sometimes feel more real than the experiences we have while awake. Many times I awoke from a nightmare and could still taste the air from the place I had just envisioned or heard the music from other realms. I knew I had just been asleep but the memory of the girl was real. I knew she had just touched me and I could still feel her hand on my forehead. All of my senses were alive and I was starting to question them as this was way beyond belief. I could not shake the thought of watching myself and the girl from the corner.

Was this what they called an out-of-body experience? I had to get a hold of myself. I rubbed my eyes and looked around. I had crossed over to the other side of the same door. I was on a wooden floor that stretched down the hallway, the one I had seen through the keyhole. The stained glass was now dull, grey and lifeless. Despite the relief from being out of that place, I felt the panic growing inside. I stood up and tried to yell but was unable to utter a word.

"What about the girl?" I thought. "There was a girl!"

I was fully awake now and the details of the nightmare were fading fast.

I recalled her wearing a white dress. She was pretty, but looked tired and pale. My recall was vague. Thus far in my life, as a blooming teenager, I had not really had a girlfriend or even discovered the opposite sex, but she stirred something in me. I had an attraction to her but it was an uneasy feeling, something not quite comforting. Maybe attraction wasn't the best way to describe it.

Was I sensing her presence and she manifested in my dream? I somehow knew it was the girl I had heard laughing in the tunnel and felt she was nearby, watching. The smell from the tunnel was still on my clothes and it made me feel queasy. I stood up too quickly and almost lost my balance as the blood rushed to my head. This place did not resemble the same view from the keyhole. I could tell it was cleaner and newer than the Big House. It was cool and dark as if the electricity had been temporarily disconnected. It felt as if at any moment this place would resume normal operation and people would appear and it would be business as usual. It had a sense of occupancy. It had the same commanding architecture of the Big House but it was much larger and spacious.

This place looked more interesting than my grandparents' home. It had order, charm and more rooms to explore! I had forgotten all about the delusion and the tunnel I had arrived from, not even questioning the past as if it had never occurred. I only wanted to know where I was and whose house I was in.

I started down the long hallway which must have had at least ten doors along the way. At the end, I could tell that it opened up into a big room like a foyer or grand entrance. If this was the entrance, I was definitely not in the Big House.

As I made my way down the corridor, a huge chandelier came into view. It was illuminated slightly as if on a dimmer and was the only source of light. Directly in front of me were two huge double doors that seemed at least 20 feet tall and the same in width. The light from the grand fixture started growing in intensity, enough so I could see the furnishings on and along the walls.

On my right side there was a table with a huge mirror above it. As I passed, I saw my reflection and was not surprised to see that I was a mess. I had dirt on my face and my shirt was torn. And there was blood on my shoulder.

"Had I fallen in the tunnel?" I questioned. As I recalled the girl touching my hair, I raised my hand and wiped my head to find blood there as well. Then I heard a cry, more like quiet sobbing. It was the girl and her sobs were coming from upstairs. I paused to listen then headed for the stairs, timidly stretching my voice but not too loud as I was not secure in this place.

"Hello, can you hear me? Are you OK? Where are you? I am coming to help you," I almost whispered.

As I came into the main area, I noticed the walls. Long curtains like sashes hung from the ceiling along the walls. They were a ruby color with a velvet texture and looked thick and heavy. To the right, a passageway curved around and disappeared down another hallway. The huge doors were directly in front of me now and towered over me. I was drawn to the staircase on my left in the direction of the voice.

I started up the stairs and felt an instant flash of déjà vu. I tried to recall the events that led me here but my head hurt with the effort. My mind would only allow me slight familiarity and a renewed sense of adventure. What a grand and mysterious house.

Fighting Fear

In my mind, fear of "the known" has always trumped fear of the unknown because of the real probability that these things can actually happen. I never wasted too much time worrying about ghosts, werewolves or vampires. I was much more terrified of things like tornados, earthquakes, lightning strikes, sharks, snakes and Sasquatch because as far as I knew, they were all real.

Residing in the Appalachians with many miles of uncharted wilderness, it was entirely possible that there was a half-man, half-beast called Sasquatch that lived in the woods. When the commercials would come on the TV advertising the movie, "The Legend of Bigfoot," I would close my eyes and beg for someone to change the channel. The fact that our house backed up to the forest didn't help. Just the thought of this huge hairy creature lurking outside my window, watching and waiting to jump out of the bushes and attack made it real and I was convinced it was out there looking in on me. Once my imagination took over, panic was not far behind.

The other huge fear I had was being beat-up by the Hopkins boys. Ever since that day at school, when they cornered me outside the auditorium, I learned to keep my distance from them. They surrounded me and I had nowhere to run. Johnny the youngest of the Hopkins boys was in my face telling me he was going to kick my ass and begging me to hit him, but I could not even though he was my age. I was paralyzed with the fear of receiving the first punch. Besides, if I did his brothers would probably jump in. So I just stood there frozen and got it, the first punch from Johnny. After that it all happened so fast. The next thing I remember was a teacher breaking up the fight and dragging Johnny and me to the principal's office. The other bullies had scattered like flies.

"Who won?" I asked the teacher as she was escorting us both up the hall and all the kids were looking at us. I looked over at Johnny and he had a bloody nose.

I thought, "Did I do that?" Wow! I didn't even try! The pride of not being such a wimp was enough for me. I did some damage. There were no marks on my face! It made me realize that the initial moments of confrontation are the hardest to get through. Once you have one foot forward the rest just flows. One only needs the confidence necessary to take that first step and know that after the initial impact you are going to be fine.

When it came to the Hopkins brothers, I was never scared when I was with Steve. But nevertheless, when we went on regular hiking or biking expeditions in the woods behind the track, we always kept our eyes peeled. Of course when we were on bikes, we could outrun them. One advantage we had was maneuverability. There was no obstacle we could not overcome and no trap we could not get out of in the woods. This was our domain and we knew every inch of the landscape.

A few months back, we were approached by Eugene, Bobby and Johnny in the woods. We just sat there on the rock up on a steep hill and displayed ourselves as easy prey. We waited until they were no more than 20 steps away and Steve yelled, "Now!" The huge old log we had been resting our feet on was just loose enough for us to push free from a ledge with our legs. We howled as it rolled down the hill after them, big and long and fast enough to make them squeal like little girls as they turned and ran for their lives. By the time they made it back up the trail to retaliate, we were long gone.

We had several outposts for taking cover. There was an ancient oak along the road that had a large hollow side perfect for hiding. There were boulders and embankments. More often than not, when it came to a choice of fight or flight it was best to get out of there. The element of surprise was one thing we held with pride and they hated us for that. We could disappear like ghosts in the woods. It was these experiences that taught me to endure and control my fear prior to the moments of impending conflict and trust that I would be OK.

"I have no fear of the unknown," I kept repeating to myself as I slowly walked up the stairs, taking in every inch of my new surroundings. For some reason, this house was not as creepy as the Big House I knew. The urgency to get out of the house had not come to me yet. On the contrary, this place was new and exciting and the beginning of a journey. In the back of my mind I thought of the girl I had seen in my dream.

No matter how frightening the concept of the ghost girl was, I was fully aware that when the time came I would deal with that fear just like a first punch. After all she was just a girl. For now, the thrill of exploration was controlling me but I had an uneasy feeling that there was something more and it was challenging my beliefs.

The ceiling on the first floor must have been at least 100 feet high. The curved staircase was long and it seemed like I was taking forever to get there. As I finally reached the landing to the second floor I noticed the lions' heads on the banisters which were identical to the ones at the foot of the stairs. The detail was incredible. Their manes were carved with fine flowing lines, their eyes almost sparkled, and they looked ready to come alive at any moment.

Letting the beasts go from my vision, I leaned over the banister and gazed at the magnificent chandelier. It was made of thousands of crystals and had flame-shaped bulbs all around. From the chandelier's gold base, "branches" with golden leaves reached toward the ceiling. It was not turned on as I originally assumed, but light shining across it from the second floor windows produced a mirror-ball effect on the foyer below.

There was no dust. Everything looked vintage but clean. Was I in a hotel? This place was much more expansive. It reminded me of a labyrinth. Every time I returned my focus on a certain aspect of the house it seemed to have changed or become more complex in its layout.

I dismissed this as an illusion every time it occurred to me, trying to remain focused on my current position. Why couldn't I remember how I got here? Every time I allowed myself to think back and tried to recall my path, I was stricken with pain. Dizzy, I grasped the banister and sat down as I reached the landing to avoid falling back down the stairs. As I sat there, I tried again to figure out where I was, but the pain in my head became overwhelming. What if someone or something was controlling my thoughts? Maybe I was a part of some mind control experiment. In my current state, I could not find any other explanation.

Suddenly, a door down the hall slowly opened with a loud creak that echoed through the house. The sound startled me so badly I jumped, my leg slipped off the top step and I teetered, trying not to slip back down the stairs. The doors to this room looked just like the ones to the treasure room in the Big House where I had found the saxophone. For a moment I was sure I was in the Big House again and that sense of familiarity gave me a flicker of hope, but then it was gone as I gazed again and everything distorted with more detail.

The door closest to the stairs was opened just enough to reveal a partial view of the room. This could not have been the Big House as the room was set up as a parlor. Cushioned chairs and a petite coffee table were centered on a fireplace, where a roaring fire burned! Fine bone china teacups on the table were half full of hot tea.

"Maybe there was an accident or the fire alarm had just gone off to cause the patrons evacuate. No one would leave a fire unattended in a house," I surmised. The room was the exact dimensions of Papa Joe's treasure room. There was no fireplace from what I could recall, but there had been too much junk packed into the room to notice. The crown molding in this room was exactly the same as what I had seen at the Big House.

"This must be the Big House but only from a dream," I thought. "This is all a dream," I half-convinced myself. I was getting dizzy again and realized I was hungry. There were funny looking cookies that were more like biscuits arranged on a platter on the coffee table. I stumbled quickly around the chair closest to the fireplace and sat down. It was an elegant chair and very comfortable. I hastily gobbled three cookies.

"Maybe they are crumpets," I thought. Having never seen a crumpet but knowing that they were served with tea, I assumed I was correct. "How fancy. Tea and crumpets by the fire. Is it teatime?" I giggled, enjoying the façade. I was having my own mad tea party! The fire was warm and my stomach welcomed the nourishment of the pastries. As my feet dangled from the chair, I looked around the room taking in the silver, china and all the other fancy arrangements. Above the fireplace was a painting of a very distinguished gentleman in his late 50's. He looked a bit like Papa Joe and I immediately thought of the saxophone.

If this was the same room, where was my saxophone? If this was not the same room of my family's house, why did the picture so closely resemble my grandfather? I wanted desperately to know what was going on! The sole fact that the saxophone might be part of a hallucination and not real was disheartening. Electric pain shot up the back of my neck again and struck me so hard I dropped the teacup. It bounced off the coffee table and hit the floor where it shattered.

I was embarrassed and ashamed as if someone would walk in at any moment and scold me for breaking their fine china. I quickly bent over to pick up the pieces. As I leaned over, dizziness overcame me again and I slipped off the chair and slammed my left temple on the side of the table. Another brilliant display of lights like those from the stained glass door flooded my vision and I was rendered unconscious on the floor over the broken china.

The Tour

"I am so sorry for your mishap," she said. "I hope you will recover. That was a nasty spill you had. Are you ill?" she asked from the chair across the coffee table. I could not utter a sound. The sight of this ghost girl sitting there in front of me was unsettling to say the least. Then I looked down and saw a body lying below me. This was even more alarming. Terror flashed through me as I realized it was my own body sprawled out on the floor, unconscious. It was like waking up to find myself trapped in a coffin and suddenly realizing there was no way out. I was having an out-of-body experience again!

I just sat there frozen in the chair, staring at the young girl and my lifeless body. She was having a cup of tea and was properly seated as if this was her afternoon ritual. She spoke casually but with a crisp British accent. I tried to speak but words were not reaching my lips. I felt a stinging sensation in the left side of my head and again and the carousel of lights danced overhead like fireflies. The room was bright, making my eyes watery and hard to focus.

"I must be asleep," I rationalized. "If I am not, what is my body doing down there?" There was no way of explaining this and admitting it allowed me the freedom to escape my inner cynic and engage in conversation with the girl. "Who are you and where am I?" I asked, finally finding the courage to speak. "Why am I here?"

"I am not quite sure," she replied very courteously. "But it is such a pleasure to have someone join me for teatime. It gets a trifle boring having tea alone. Won't you please have some?"

"I don't think so," I spouted off, angry at how nonchalant she was about the situation. "I need some answers! You have been following me because I heard you in the tunnel and I saw you downstairs in the same state I am in now, asleep or something? Why is my body on the floor? Is this my grandparents' house?"

"You would do well to mind your manners. I am being cheery with you and would expect you to do the same. There is no need to raise your voice," she replied delicately but firmly. "To your questions, I am not sure where you came from or how you got here. You must be joking about a body on the floor. Are you mocking me or just trying to frighten me?"

The girl paused to allow me to answer, and when I did not, she continued. "I am only happy to have a visitor. It has been quite awhile since I had someone to play with. Please allow me to introduce myself. My name is Claudia. I live here in the house. It is a magnificent house, don't you think? I have so much to show you. Would you like a tour?"

This very self-assured mannerly girl was really unaware of what was happening to me and that made two of us. I must be asleep or unconscious from the fall, I reasoned. It took a moment but my faculties came back into focus.

I could remember bits and pieces again. I could not tell dreams from reality at this point but I was able to recall what had happened to me recently. I recalled staring at the Big House, noticing the open door and running in to check for the burglary of my prized saxophone. I remembered running up the stairs, falling into the bowels of something alive and the long climb out of the tunnel which had transformed itself into a staircase. I had heard this girl's voice twice while I was awake, and after, had seen her twice now that I was beside myself (literally). She must be a dream, I concluded. If she was not a ghost, then I was not in harm's way. All I had to do was wake up and she would be gone.

But my curiosity dominated and the explorer in me spoke up before I had a chance to challenge my instincts. "Yes I would love a tour of this grand old establishment," I responded slightly mocking her but more so, trying to accommodate her, to figure out where I was and what was happening to me.

I consider myself very good at adapting to new environments. I try to refrain from being too much of a "nice guy" but find myself doing so every time. Being over-accommodating with people almost always leaves me vulnerable and often taken for granted. In spite of this, within only a few minutes of meeting and spending some time with someone, I can make a connection with almost anyone. In the past, I've proved an uncanny ability to relate to others. I always feel the need to make people feel comfortable and at ease. Did that make me a giving person? I don't ever recall being able to do this on purpose, like when I needed to. It came naturally and made it easy for most to be themselves around me.

At this point in the conversation with this ghost of a girl in my dreams, I was hopeful to have some knowledge, any knowledge of how I got here even though I wasn't quite sure where "here" was. My thrill for adventure was returning and I was willing to allow this dainty young girl to give me a formal tour. With a guide, I would now be able to get more insight into this place as it was unfolding around me.

She stood up from her chair and proceeded around the coffee table towards me. I was surprised by how she moved, more floating across the carpet than walking. "I am definitely not awake," I told myself in an effort to not be consumed by the fear that she may indeed be a ghost. As she rounded the table, she was about to step on my body but instead was able to hover over it without realizing there was a "physical" version of me on the floor. This was the second time I had seen her and she was obviously not aware of her spiritual condition. I dared not enlighten her now.

"I want to show you my quarters in the back of the house where my family stays," she said, her voice full of pride. "We must hurry. My parents are coming home soon and it will be time for dinner. Would you like to join us?"

She quickly grabbed my hand.

I felt her cool flesh in mine and it sent a shiver through my body. It was like she was pulling the warmth and life from me. I pulled my hand out of her grip and she snapped her head to face me. "Is there a problem?" she asked, a little coldly.

I didn't want to tell her I was afraid she was a ghost and replied, "I am a little shy."

"Think nothing of it," she responded, defensively. "Let's go downstairs and I will show you the back of the house where I live." We exited the room that resembled Papa Joe's junk room and walked to the stairs. In an effort to gain Claudia's trust, I took her again hand despite my fears. It was still clammy and cold but I disregarded the sensation.

She looked at me and her eyes changed. They were a beautiful green color and I suddenly realized that I had been seeing everything in black and white, or rather, shades of grey. She smiled tenderly and said, "You never told me your name."

As I was looking at her deep green eyes they quickly dissolved back into a grey tone. My eyes were playing tricks on me. I did not allow this to distract me as I wanted to make sure I did not offend Claudia. I was in her world now and was sure that she had all the control. "My name is Andy." I said. "It's my pleasure. My grandparents own this house and I am just looking around. This is a wonderful place with so many great secrets waiting to be discovered."

"Indeed it is," she replied with a slight reluctance in her voice.

She led me to the stairs where the massive lion heads rested on the banisters. They seemed less vicious now and appeared more as proud guardians. No longer tempted to turn my gaze, I was drawn to their firm and gracious stare with the feeling that I was protected.

As we descended the long winding staircase, she began her narration. "My family has lived here for many years. My father is the groundskeeper and my mother, the maid. I have not yet spoken to the owners of the house as I am forbidden to do so and usually stay in the servants' quarters unless I am helping my parents serve or clean. They would be dreadfully upset to know I was in the main part of the house by myself. It is forbidden for us to be here unless we are serving or cleaning. But I was compelled to meet you in hopes that you would come and play with me. I was waiting for my parents to return and became bored. They would fancy meeting you, Master Andy and would be delighted if you stayed for dinner."

The main foyer had not changed since I arrived although it seemed a bit darker. The light no longer shone on the crystal chandelier. The sparkle was gone and the place looked dreary and spooky. I imagined it was late in the afternoon. Everything was laid out similar to the Big House but somehow opposite, and much larger in scale.

There was no front door where it was supposed to be; only a huge double door without windows. The corridor opposite the landing was similar to the den in The Big House that led to the dining room. We reached the landing and went right, heading back towards the stained glass where I had arrived from the basement. As we passed down the long hallway, I glanced in the mirror, which now was on my left side and was caught by the sight of blood on my head and shoulder.

"Wait," I said, my voice shrill. "Earlier when I looked in the mirror I saw blood on the right side of my head. Now it is on my left. I am sure of this!" It was as if I was seeing the mirror image of my earlier self. She pretended not to know anything about it and pulled my arm. "Mirrors play tricks on the eye. When we get to our quarters, I will tend to your head," she said attentively but not quite as sincere, attempting to distract me from my discovery. "Come this way, I can't wait to show you my room."

As we continued I felt a warm sensation surge through my body and I could have sworn I heard whispers, the way my mother would say "goodnight" before tucking us in at bedtime. It was immediately followed by chills. "Did you hear that?" I asked.

"Hear what?" Claudia responded.

"Never mind," I said, trying to keep my growing paranoia hidden. As we got closer, the stained glass was now a cold dark grey. "We shouldn't go this way," I protested. "This is the place I came from and it leads to the basement."

My recollection of events was fading fast and my short-term memory was totally out of whack.

All I could recall was steps leading down to a basement that had once been a tunnel.

"Don't be silly, you must have been lost. This is the way to the staffs' quarters," she replied, trying to disguise the fact that she knew she had met me in this very spot earlier. "This house is so big it is easy to get confused and many places look the same," she continued. She knew I was not falling for that. I was sure of my location and that I'd been here earlier.

"This house was designed by expert builders that came from London and there are many secret passageways and doors. I will show you some of them later. That is the fun part," she said with a seemingly unintentional lower pitch in her voice that reminded me of the butler from the Adam's Family. What was her idea of fun …killing me?

As she continued to describe details of the home during our stroll, I found Claudia to be a clever conversationalist. She had a certain deceitful charm that allowed her to compliment you, tap into your true desires and ultimately have her way. Although I was aware of her ability to distract and manipulate, I was also completely taken by the notion of secret passageways and hidden chambers she was describing that were used primarily as short cuts for the staff.

I was, however, very fearful of being trapped back in that tunnel and I didn't want her to notice my hesitance.

As we approached the stain glass door, I slowed my pace and fell back ever so slightly so she wouldn't catch me squatting to see through the keyhole. There was very dim light, but I could not focus enough to see what was on the other side. That was good enough for me, as I recalled from being on the other side that there was no light at all. I was just curious.

"My father once told me that the light through a keyhole is the same light that shines from your soul," she said pretending not to see me secretly glancing. "It is a symbol of hope."

Great! If I saw no light through my keyhole, was I dead? I was becoming nervous as this tour proceeded, but my curiosity would not allow me to give into my fears and we proceeded down the eternal hallway.

Besides, what choice did I have? I was lost.

The Dark Side

"This is where I live," she said, guiding me through a door that led down another dark hallway which formed an "L" shape. There were four doors along the hallway ahead of the bend and one of them led to a moderately lit room. This area of the house was less ornate, almost ordinary, and the ceilings were not as high as the rest of the house. The walls were plain and had no fancy trim along the ceiling. There was a bitter odor that I could not describe nor had I ever encountered before and it brought to mind death. I did not have a good feeling about this part of the house and tried to recall what Papa Joe had said about the servants' quarters when giving me my initial tour. My mind could not retrieve his description, except for that one word, death. Had someone died here?

I felt the pain rising to my head once again and stopped trying to remember. "My room is over here. Please excuse the clutter. I must clean it before my parents arrive. I want to show you something," she said excitedly. Near the end of the hall where I could see more light, it looked like a kitchen but she grabbed my hand and led me to a room on the right; her room.

The stench was worse in here and I tried to ignore it, trying not to be obvious by holding my nose. Inside the room was a plain small bed. It was made properly with old yellowing white sheets but I could see the imprints left by the last person who laid there. There were regular windows with curtains covering them. There was faint light coming through. I had the urge to peek out the windows to see what part of house we were in as I knew every inch of the grounds surrounding the Big House. But, before I could do so, she pulled me away toward the corner of her room beyond the bed.

"This is my doll collection. These were my mother's and some were her mother's." The dolls were nicely lined up on a dresser in front of a mirror. I was distracted by our reflection. There were indeed two reflections, but the image returned of Claudia was discolored. She looked half grey and half green. I didn't look that good myself after being in this dusty old house all day.

"The one on my left is a gift from my father. He gave me this doll on my 8th birthday," she said, adoring her little treasure. "Isn't she grand?"

I nodded in agreement. Dolls weren't really my cup of tea. It was a nice collection though. They all had ceramic heads, hands and feet and what appeared to be real hair. The paintings on the faces were very detailed and had bright colors that made the dolls seem alive and real. Her favorite doll, the one she was pointing to, keenly resembled Claudia. The eyes were large and green and had a glossiness that made them look very deep.

"Why, Claudia" I said in a surprised tone, "This doll is you!"

I could tell that she was impressed by the fact that I noticed and for a second her eyes looked like the doll.

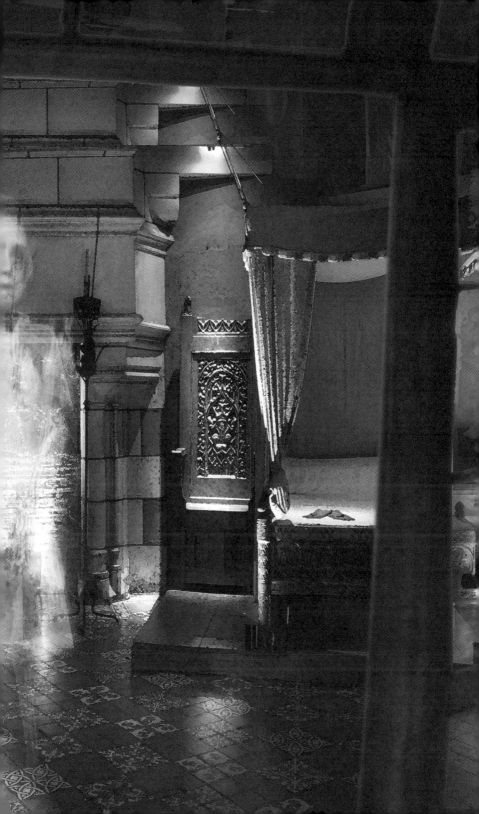

Her own eyes were bright green again, just like when I had seen them the first time. It was as if there was a small Christmas bulb behind each of them and I had just hit the switch.

"'Your eyes just changed Claudia," I exclaimed with bewilderment. She totally ignored my statement and quickly changed the subject. "You noticed! My father saw it one day in an antique shop and bought it for the same reason." I could tell that this was her prized possession, like the saxophone was to me. When she looked at it she appeared to feel secure, warm and full of hope and inspiration.

I was beginning to grow fond of Claudia. She was sweet and being that this was my first friend that was a girl, I had no problems talking with her about dolls even though they weren't very interesting for me. She was a special person. I could tell. Her mannerisms were subtle and her demeanor was kind. I relaxed and felt a bit ashamed for my earlier paranoia. As I looked at the dolls again, pretending to be interested, my mind once again insisted on questioning my predicament.

I was expecting that pain to return that was more like a pressure or weight on my skull. It didn't come.

"Why am I here? Who is this girl and where are her parents? Why is she in this house? Is she really a ghost?" As these questions raced through my mind, I felt a sense of danger. I glanced past the dolls to the mirror. Claudia was standing right beside me but was not in the reflection. I felt someone on the bed behind me. It was twilight in the room now, but I could instantly recognize that it was a dead body, Claudia's body! Her corpse was way past rigor mortis and almost nothing but a skeleton and hair remained. As the stench became overwhelming, I tried to scream but I could not.

Time trapped me in the mirror and I was frozen there as I felt the uncontrollable sense of floating. I could not turn around to validate this view. I did not want to see her like this. I could not turn to run either. I was unable to move, my mind paralyzed by what I was seeing.

When I finally had enough control of my body to respond, I screamed at the top of my lungs, "I want out of here. I want to go home! Mom!"

Free Will

I had a dream I was flying, the wind lifting me up, up, up and then I would float for awhile as I scanned the woodlands below. I was soaring alongside a ridge. I could see two motorcycles screaming down the old dirt road. My first thought was of my brother, Ben on his little Green Machine, one of those bikes like Steve's made for motocross.

It was just another day in paradise. I recalled that feeling of total freedom and having nothing to do but ride. My mind was wide open, full of hope and the spirit of adventure. Lifted higher by the breeze, I could now see over the ridge and along the road that ran behind our house. I could see my house. The feeling was incredible! I was drifting effortlessly and the view was grand. My vision then shifted to a blazing carousel of lights. The colors originated from one bright source of white light. I wanted to fly in that direction.

As I gazed into the light, the pain in my head arrested my senses and the colors dimmed. As my body wrestled for control of my mind, I felt pressure on the left side of my face. My vision corrected and I gradually left my grand flight to realize I was face down on the floor. Little white triangles around faded purple and red paisley shapes stretched in front of me. I was on a carpet. My head ached and my arm was numb from where I had been lying on top of it. As I came to, I recalled the girl's body on the bed, long since dead. Fresh terror ran through me.

I pushed myself to all fours and grabbed the table to help me to my feet. The world was spinning and I knew now that none of this was real. Just where was I? The last thing I remember was the horrific vision of Claudia's rotting corpse, but I tried to console myself that it was all just a dream.

"Get a hold of yourself," I demanded of my faculties. As I tried to grasp where I was now, I noticed two things. The fireplace had no fire and the lights were on in the house, as if in full operation. My only question was, "Am I still in the same room, the same house?" It was changing so fast I was not sure of anything anymore, except for this: I did not want to see Claudia again.

I was now a believer in ghosts and my spirit for adventure had been lessened by the reality of the world she had shown me. I was not interested in knowing more. I just wanted to go home. Now, as I looked around almost certainly the same parlor room where I had just had a tea party with a ghost, it was as if I had never left this room, had never seen the dead girl, or that someone had carried me back here, afterwards.

The room was joyous and new details came to light. Fancy gold trim edged the ceilings and the little baby angels in the woodwork seemed happy, almost smiling. While I felt the renewed desire to explore this incredible house, the recollection of the scene in Claudia's room lingered around me. I tried to shake the images from my thoughts.

Even though she was a ghost, she was nice to me and I was curious about her. Was she trying to tell me something? Did the house have a dark side? Might I end up in a more dangerous and ominous place than the dark dungeon of a tunnel? My world was no longer the same since I had met Claudia. I realized I was actually concerned for her. In her normal state she appeared innocent and lost. Pushing all this aside in my head, I took a deep breath and headed for the door. My curiosity had prevailed again but now my guard was up.

As I walked out of the parlor to the upper landing, I started back down the hallway. The upstairs obviously was where the proprietors of the house had their master bedrooms. The other doors were not of the type that slid apart like in the parlour. They came in pairs, side by side like in hotels with adjoining rooms. At the first door on the right, I leaned down and peeked into the keyhole. There was some light on the other side but nothing spectacular, much better than darkness. I decided to be brave and reached for the tarnished doorknob which was shaped like a flower. I turned the knob and entered.

As I did, I heard Claudia moaning and whispering from down the hall. I was not ready to face her again and ducked into the room.

Mother's Secret

Ayoung girl must have lived here as there was a canopy bed topped with a frilly bedspread. The room had a warm glow about it and as I looked around at the décor I felt safe. In the corner there was a vanity with a round mirror and a chair. On the vanity was a silver brush tarnished with age. I turned it over and could see traces of a handprint in slightly green oxidation from the girl who last used it, the imprint encapsulated in time. As I stared at this relic, I thought of my mother.

Mom was always good to my siblings and me. I remembered Saturday mornings as the best of times. "Kids, get up. Breakfast will be ready soon," my mother would call. My brother and I would rise to the smell of bacon and eggs and would race down the hall, switch on the TV to watch our favorite cartoons. She would let us sleep in if we chose, but we didn't want to miss a moment of the weekend time. Sometimes she would even let us eat our cereal on the couch, but when breakfast was served she demanded we gather together as a family at the table. On school days, if we woke to snow on the lawn, we would anxiously listen to the radio and pray school was closed. On these precious days, the golden words of the disc jockey announcing school closings were nothing short of magic. The kids next door and all throughout the neighborhood would be doing the same thing, thrilled by the opportunity to play all day.

After breakfast, Mom helped us get ready, putting on our socks and pulling them snuggly up our legs so there were no wrinkles. If left to dress ourselves, we would throw on our clothes as fast as we could and come back inside 20 minutes later freezing. She would then add layer upon layer of pants and shirts and socks upon us until we were three times our actual size. Before we could get out the door again we were sweating. Once suited up, we would spend hours outside until we heard her calling from the back door for a hot chocolate break.

As I contemplated my mother and our home, I felt lonely. I missed being home and wanted to get back there, but somehow I felt her presence and the feeling passed. "This must have been her room," I thought, surprised that it had taken me so long to make the connection. "This is where she grew up! And that must be her handprint on the brush." Excitement surged through me and brought a chill as I looked around the room for familiar reminders of things my mother cherished. I was comforted by the confirmation that I was back in the Big House.

On the right side of the vanity was a tiny crystal sculpture of an angel. She always liked these figurines and this passion of hers must have started here, maybe even with this crystal being her first, I surmised. Imagining my mother as a young girl was strange as she was always my mother. "This is where she spent her days as a kid my age," I thought and resumed my investigation.

In the corner of the room, adjacent to the bed was a

huge case with glass doors. This must have been her precious collection. There were more crystal figurines and dolls. The dolls were familiar, but at first glance I could not recall why. Then it hit me. Claudia's doll collection. It seemed as if I had seen it a long time ago. My sense of time was all screwed up.

"This is just a dream," I said out loud just to hear myself speak. "I must be creating all this in my mind." After the last visit to the Big House, I found myself wildly alive with the thrill of discovery. Somehow I must have taken this experience and incorporated it into my subconscious. This rationalization set me at ease and calmed my fears. I had no problem with letting the dream unravel on its own. I could endure ghosts and haunted houses until forced awake with a cold sweat and only the memories of fear and death. I did not want this reverie to end and instead kept my attention on the wonders of this place. The glass would remain half full until I got back to the room where the saxophone awaited rescue.

The dolls in the case were much more modern and more expensive than Claudia's, although they were of the same type. Their ceramic faces were exquisitely painted and must have been worth much money. The dresses were trimmed in shiny material like gold. Their little shoes were made of fine leather and some even had ballerina shoes. They even looked like they had real teeth and eyes.

"Did they come from real little babies?" I thought and it gave me a chill and a giggle all at once.

Nah, that would be cruel. But the detail of each doll was amazing. I wondered why my mother did not take this fine collection with her. I remembered the doll Claudia's father had bought for her and how she told the story with such enthusiasm. Her dolls had more raggedy clothing, but she was so proud of them. Claudia's green, glowing eyes came back to me.

Claudia had been charming and entertaining when she was in her little girl form. Still, to take on a ghost for a companion was alarming. Even if I perceived her as a ghost, she was someone to talk to, someone to share this adventure. I was becoming aware of the fact that the house had stories I may not want to know, and that perhaps Claudia knew them all to well.

"Everything has its good side and bad," I justified. In doing so I was testing my strength, courage and ingenuity. I would rather be at risk with her, than remain alone here. Conspiring with a ghost was better than living inside myself with all these questions and fears. Nevertheless, it didn't matter. I was only hallucinating and she was not real.

Somehow I knew better. She felt real, she looked real and somehow she was a part of this house. "As soon as I wake up from this dream, I will go back into the house to try and reach her spirit," I thought, not entirely convinced that I wanted to or would even be able to remember.

I went back to my inspection of what I was calling my mother's room. On the other side of the bed was a window. There was a rocking chair beside it in the corner between the wall and the nightstand. As with most of the rooms of the house, the fancy wall trim intrigued me. In each corner of the bedroom along the ceiling, were figurines and faces carved into the rich dark wood millwork. Their eyes seemed to follow me around the room wherever I went. When the light was right, it was comforting and attractive, but in the shadows the faces seemed ominous and threatening.

I took another look at the vanity and opened the top drawer. It was lined with red velvet and had the same distinct smell as the inside of the saxophone case, a musty and spicy aroma, composed of oils and dust from the people, places and things it had been in proximity with throughout the years. It was the smell of history.

I pulled the drawer all the way out and it slipped from its groove, sending the contents crashing to the floor. There was a key, a letter and a few other items I disregarded as junk. The letter was on parchment paper and was folded two ways but I was able to see through it enough to realize it was handwritten in ink. I opened it and instantly recognized my mother's handwriting. Neat cursive with a little loop around the Ts.

"Her handwriting is exactly the same today as it was then," I exclaimed, which really made me miss her. "She would have been about my age! This was a letter that she actually wrote!" The ink was only slightly faded but the paper was yellow on the edges, fragile and ready to crumble. It read:

The Ghosts of Virginia

For centuries people have tried to make exploratory invasions into the world of the unknown. Almost every society known has some belief in "Survival after Death." Christian ideas about the afterlife include an assignment to either Heaven or Hell, depending on one's merits. The Zulus, in Africa, believe in an underworld, where below the earth, there are mountains and villages where the dead live. And despite the differences in beliefs, both have much in common; they share the belief of communication between the living and the dead. Many legends have been preserved and passed down from generation to generation. For whatever reason, these ghostly treasures have survived so that others may experience the thrill of the strange, the unexplained and the mystic.

What exactly is a ghost?

Virginia has had it's share of tragedy like horrible famines, Indian massacres, the Revolutionary War, the Civil War and countless stories of grieving, suffering and dying that accompanied these events.

Being the oldest colony in the New World, Virginia has a richer, longer history that dates back for centuries. The travesty of death has diverted many mortal viewpoints far from the material world and forced them to look at the miracle of life with more profound adoration. Maybe that is how they coined the phrase, "Virginia is for Lovers".

It was definitely my mother's handwriting! It was obviously a rough draft and there were a few more pages but the rest was just notes and incomplete sentences. But why had she written this paper on ghosts? Maybe she had met Claudia. Maybe she was haunted by her as well.

"So Claudia is real!" It brought me chills once I said it out loud. "As real as a dream can be, I guess," I laughed nervously as I replayed the events from my fantasy in my head.

I grabbed the key and turned it over in my hand. It was a skeleton key, a master key. "But what door does it fit?" I wondered. As I moved to stand up, I heard a squeak from the other side of the room. It sounded like it was coming from the rocking chair. I was facing the vanity, my back to the rocker. I paused for a moment, half in terror and half in preparation of what I might see. The words from my mother's paper echoed in my mind. "What exactly is a ghost?" I was no longer afraid to address Claudia, the girl-ghost. If my mother could do it so could I. Whether she had actually met this ghost or not was beside the point. I had found enough words of encouragement to at least pose the question for myself. Now I wanted to know. I wanted to learn more about ghosts and specifically, Claudia. I stood up slowly and caught the view of the rocking chair in the mirror. It was Claudia, exactly as she appeared in the bed, except sitting upright. Her skeleton ricketing in the chair, loose skin falling from the bones of her hands as they propelled her motion, and she was laughing at me!

My first instinct was to blurt out a little chuckle as it slightly resembled a ghost in a cartoon as she rocked away. She was wearing the same tattered white dress her corpse was wearing when she showed me her room. The skull turned in my direction as I peered at the reflection through the mirror and her jaw gaped open. "I am bored, let's play."

It wasn't the voice of Claudia. It sounded like a monster. The voice was deep and shrill all at once. "Master Andy, play with me," it insisted. My fear returned promptly.

Ghosts didn't seem that interesting now. Breathing was my primary focus. I struggled for a breath, but my lungs wouldn't work. I started to shake and could feel the need for oxygen. I wanted to run, breathe, scream — all of the above — but stood frozen in front of the mirror.

"Turn around," I ordered myself. "She is only a ghost and I can only see her through the mirror," I was half lying to myself but with hopes that I was right. "Please!?" the ghost pleaded in an even more morbid manner. I turned around valiantly expecting to be reassured of my theory only to find the first-hand view of Claudia's decaying skeleton rocking in the chair. I reached down, grabbed the note and with the key in the other hand, I ran for it. Without even thinking, I raced for the first set of doors I could find. The room went dark and the being shrieked, sending me into a panic to find an escape. I came to a set of folding doors, opened them and ran through, only to slam my head against a shelf,

I fell to my knees behind the doors and tried to shake the painful strike to my head. I had run into a closet. "You moron!" I thought, disgusted with my gutless self. I was cowering in a closet with a monster cornering me.

"I'm trapped. I want to wake up." Two seconds passed and I realized that I should not wait for that to happen. Hands outstretched, I frantically felt my way around for something to hide behind. As I felt along the back of the closet, my balance shifted and I fell forward through a panel. It was a way out!

I scuffled down what seemed a passage away from the room and the ghost. I imagined for a second that I was the star character in a mystery movie, "The Haunted Big House." Suddenly, the fear was gone again, and I was charged with adventure once more but in a deeper, more spiritual way. I was in totally unfamiliar territory, but, somehow, it felt great! I felt her good spirit encircling me, even as the bag of bones wimpered and childed in the bedroom outside. Then the joy was gone again and I wept in unision with her corpse.

The real Claudia was coaxing me and now I would find her. My direction, whichever I chose was not of importance. I would be led back to her. I wasn't sure what I was saving her from but I was sure we'd collided for a reason. Reading the letter made me realize this had been going on for a long, long time. I was sent here to help her out of the house. I needed to locate the Claudia I first met, not her physical body, that terrifying skeleton, but her spirit. I had a mission.

The Big House

Book Two
Revival

Twin Rooms

At the age of 13, I was pretty sure of who I was and what I was capable of. I knew what made me tick and what made me happy. My interests included building things, like model cars and boats. I definitely liked the outdoor activities, music and the opportunity to share thoughts and activities with others. I wondered how much I would accomplish in life and what was my special gift?

However lacking in experience, I was still equipped with all the passion that youth preserves and my spirit was invincible. I was proud of the way I was handling this scary place for the most part, but I was not exactly thrilled with being manipulated by this ghost.

There were no colors where I was now. The space behind the closet was dark, dusty and cold. I could see light beaming through the panels in thin horizontal lines. It was very dim but consistent from the floor to the ceiling. Although the corridor was dark, I could see some light at the end to help guide me past these black voids.

"I must be near the outer edge of the house," I thought. Just the idea of being that high up from the yard made me teeter and check my balance. I tried to sketch out my position in my head. I knew I was moving along the southeast corner on the second floor. "Mother's bedroom was the second door from the stairs, so there must be one more room on the southeast corner on the other side of this wall," I reasoned.

The cobwebs were thick and damp. I wiped them from my face and proceeded forward, my right hand on the wall and my left hand in front of my face to detect obstacles, especially spider webs. About ten feet from the end, I could see a wall and a faint light source to the left around a corner. As I approached the first dark zone, I stumbled on a loose board and almost fell, fearing that I may slip between the walls to the first floor where I would end up like Claudia before anyone ever found me. I moved on much slower, feeling my way down the two-foot wide wall space careful not to scratch my hands on nails. I could not get the layout straight as I mapped out the upper level of the house in my head. I continued on, hands in front of me, guiding me along the walls. The light ahead was fading leaving me no direction or a sense of an end to this path. Fear was beginning to take over. I came to the end of the path and the only light I could see was now behind me.

"Where to now?" I was trapped! I began to feel claustrophobic and that gave my fears full reign. "Once again, I'm lost in the depths of the house, trapped by my own fear. Now I have to go back and face Claudia's ghost." That thought gave way to an overwhelming need to get out of here and to a safe place. In a panic, I started feeling my way back out and scraped my left hand on a nail. The pain consumed me and I panicked,

"Somebody help me, I'm trapped in here!" I shouted.

"Can anybody hear me? Help!" I started kicking the wall to see if I could break through.

"Is there anyone out there? Pleeeeaaase help." I was sure I would die a horrible death, stuck in this dark world all alone, never to be found. I kicked the wall in front of me and a door flew open

"That could not be. I am only half way back to the place where I entered," I thought but wasted no time, fell to my knees and crawled out hastily. I was back where I started, in the closet. I didn't have time to question how I got back so quickly; I was more concerned with the creature still being in the room. How was I to deal with Claudia's beast and get past it without a confrontation? I could burst from the closet and just run to the door and not be such a fool as to trap myself this time. I stood up and as I did, my head made contact with coat hangers and some old musty smelling clothes. My feeling of being trapped took over again and I sprung from the closet before I could remind myself of the potential danger waiting for me there. Mother's room looked different. The light was all wrong. Claudia's ghost was nowhere to be seen. I was breathing heavy and leaned over, resting my hands on my knees and tried to get a grip. There was blood on my arm from a nail I encountered and I wiped it on my filthy shirt.

This room was similar to mother's room, but at first I could not tell what was different. The same furnishings were in place, but it was like looking in a mirror. Everything in this room was flipped. "This cannot be happening. This is not real," I repeated as I tried to get perspective. Everything was opposite how I found it when I came in the room the first time. The window was on the other side of the bed. Was I seeing a reflection or was I in a different room? The rocking chair was beside the window, but was now in the opposite corner. I looked to the door and then behind me at the closet. There was no way I could have been in a passageway. The back wall of the closet would be against the parlor where I had sat and had tea by the fireplace. I walked back to the vanity, surveying the mirror-image configuration of the room I had left before entering the secret passageway.

Perhaps there had been no passageway. Maybe I was so scared I imagined it while stuck in the closet, hiding from Claudia's ghost. This is the best possible reason I could find for the situation. The glass cabinet with all the dolls was still beside the rocking chair and appeared the same. I paused as I walked toward the vanity and glanced back sharply, noticing something was different with the dolls in the collection. As I got closer I noticed they were all dressed in different styles and colors. These dolls were dressed in yellows, blues and greens. I could have sworn they were mostly white and shades of red and their eyes were different. They were lifeless and vacant.

This was no longer my mother's room as similar as it appeared. I was sure of that. I turned back to the vanity and walked to the mirror, reluctantly.

Where the crystal angel had been, there was now a glass statue of a clown. It was not a happy clown, but more stern and somber. It gave me chills.

I opened the drawer and the contents spilled to the floor as had happened only moments ago. "Oh, no here we go again," I said trying to inject some humor into the moment but only dread remained. As I kneeled to pick up the items, I only found useless miscellaneous items, dust bunnies and a comb. The drawer was not lined with the velvety soft fabric as before. It was only old wood and as I picked it up to re-insert it I caught a splinter in my right thumb. The pain felt surprisingly good as it was a sensation that was identifiable and real. Feeling more in touch with myself, I quickly slid the drawer into the groove and rose to my feet.

I was reluctant to look in the mirror, but my eyes could not avoid the view. She was not there. I sighed in relief. To the left of the mirror on the vanity was a picture that was not there before. It was a picture of a girl. She was seated and dressed in a formal gown. It was a studio portrait and she looked very pristine and poised. I had seen this picture before but could not remember where. I had to stare at it for a moment to recall where I had seen that face. It looked like my mother, but there was something different I could not identify. Her expression was not quite like the one my mother would use and her gaze was more serious. Then it came to me. "This is her twin sister, Catherine!" I was wild with excitement for my discovery. This was my aunt's room, identical but with only very slight differences. This made perfect sense but my mind would not let go of the physical layout and how I ended up here.

I returned to the closet, planning to retrace my footsteps, not really convinced I would dare go back down that secret passageway. I walked in the closet and felt along the place where I had accidentally found the secret door. I ran my hands all along the wall, moving firmly against the woodwork, pushing and banging as I went. There was no trap door! It was all my imagination. Did the ghost scare me so bad that I imagined it? Maybe my mind had invented it to protect me from the demonic vision in the rocking chair. Or maybe I would wake up soon. I was now running out of any desire to explore. The fascination of thinking there were elusive, secret paths behind these walls was gone. Conversely, I was in prison.

I wanted to put my feet back on solid ground and go home. The thrill of adventure was replaced with the fear I'd recently met. The stench returned. I still could not make sense of where I was in the house and suddenly felt the need to get back to familiar territory. I would have welcomed meeting Murphy in these creepy corridors. As I opened the door to my mother's room, I instead saw the hallway, where the ghost stood only a few feet from me, blocking my exit. It was hideous with distorted feature and when it started moving towards me and I froze, paralyzed by sheer terror. My mind was screaming "Run!" but I couldn't even breath.

The Front Line

I have always dreaded confrontations. A flood of emotions courses through me as my mind struggles between my subconscious and conscious demands. War is waged internally as fear and faith stand face to face. The dilemma: leap forward with nothing but courage and faith or turn to run in fear.

This was never my best department. I usually got way too nervous during these critical moments and my mind would freeze in fear of the outcome. But the moment had come again and this time I put one shaking foot forward.

"Who are you and where is Claudia?" I demanded, my voice trembling. The ghost was three feet in front of me and blocking my path out of the room.

"What do you want from me?" I asked. The room started changing colors. Beams of metallic light emanated from this being and illuminated the room around us. The rest of the room went pitch dark as if all light and energy was flowing into the ghost. I could see a resemblance of Claudia as the body formed an outline over her skeleton. It was almost like looking at a hologram but the skeletal remains were solid and real and you could not see through them.

"What are you doing in this house?" the ghost inquired sternly. It had no eyes but as the demon spoke the sockets glowed a bright, electric kind of green. I had seen a glimpse of this in Claudia's eyes when we were in her bedroom.

Claudia's eyes, the real Claudia's, were captivating and beautiful. The creature before me had eyes that were haunting and hollow, yet, I found myself unable to turn away.

I summoned up the courage to ask the question to which I already knew the answer. "Are you Claudia? I want to talk with Claudia." I had learned this from some movie about exorcism. I was hoping to reach the nicer side of the ghost. There was no response but the glow in the eyes subsided. "Why are you playing tricks on me? Why are you here? I need to know what happened to Claudia."

"You will stay here with us. There are many things we want to show you," said the figure. It started to rise, hovering slightly above me. I realized I must get free from it and try to find the real Claudia. Before I had a chance to act, the ghost extended its arms and unleashed a horrid wail. It would not let me pass. I wanted to run and hide. There was no more thrill in this place and the treasure I was so desperately seeking was far from my thoughts. Besides, I was so cold that I could see my breath. Panic was the only emotion I could feel and it surged through my body: so much for having courage and spirit. I had been robbed of that and was no longer equipped with a sense of humanity for poor Claudia. I just wanted out of this terrible place. Cornered by this ghost, I scrunched my hands down in my pockets to keep warm and the head pain returned.

"I still have the key," I said to myself, gripping it tightly, as if the creature were not right there before me. "If I can make it back to Claudia's room I may be able to reason with her to make the ghost leave me alone." I wanted out in the worst way. The ghost picked up on my intentions.

"You cannot leave here!" the being wailed. "You came here and now you must stay," said the dark spirit. That was all I needed to hear. No longer able to rationalize, I was back in fight or flight mode. I kept my right hand in my pocket holding onto the key as if it was my only savior. I slid my left hand from my pocket and felt the wall behind me. There was a light switch. The room had grown dark but I did not remember the lights ever being on. Yet it seemed only minutes ago, the house was full of light, warm and inviting. The ghost was playing with my mind and thoughts.

"I am actually in control here," I tried desperately to convince myself. I realized that every time I felt bested and wanted to leave, the place was cold and dark and the ghost was angry. As I had regained some of my spirit and courage, the ghost acted against my will to beat me back down. That is why I was frightened into the closet, only to be trapped in another dead end. If that was the case, maybe I could trick the ghost. It was worth a try so I would play its little game.

"What else do you want to show me?" I asked. "You already showed me a secret passageway but that was a trick. Take me to Claudia and I will stay here with you. Then you can show me anything you like." It had worked! The ghost had recognized my surrender and believed I was not going to try to leave.

The eerie glow in its eyes softened. I leaned against the wall and put my hand on the light switch. I flipped the switch and the light came on instantly, filling the room. The ghostly image dissipated enough so I could barely see the holographic body and the skeleton had turned slightly translucent. The green glow from the eye sockets was gone. The being had lost its grip on me, controlling me with its fearful image. I took off for the door, passing straight through the being. I had expected to feel the impact of its bony body, but there was nothing but a cold chill. I raced out of the room and down the hall back toward the stairs. The ghost wailed and the house shook violently. Above me, I heard hissing noises. The cherubs along the ceiling had changed. They were transforming into gargoyles and were coming alive! They stretched their wings from the woodwork, ready to fly down and attack me. Their eyes lit up in an angry red glow.

As I reached the stairway, all at once the lions' heads that rested on the banisters came to life and unleashed a roar that rattled me to the core. I took the stairs two and three at once, not concerned with losing my balance and falling. I turned to glance behind me and what I saw turned simple fear into terror. They were rising straight out of the banister rail; their front legs reaching the floor and their bodies emerging from the posts. They roared again, rocking the chandelier above and charged toward me. I was almost down to the first floor now and moving at full speed when I tripped. Instead of taking the fall, I lurched forward clearing the last two stairs and rolled skillfully back onto my feet, a performance befitting a gymnast. I rounded the corner and sprinted down the hall until my legs burned. I could hear the animals descending the stairs behind me but I didn't dare look back. No matter how hard I tried I could not pick up the pace. The carpet felt as if it was being reeled up beneath me. Despite my failing momentum, I warned myself I would be defeated if the ghost sensed my fears.

"Don't believe in this, it isn't real. It's all a trick. Just run!" The beasts were gaining on me. I had made it to the end of the very long hall and past the basement passage, the stain glass, and toward the servants' wing. I looked back in time to see one of the lions take the corner too fast and crash into the basement door. It roared in anger and pain as the second lion careened into it as well. They scrambled to get back in motion while growling and swatting at each other. I was going to make it.

I found Claudia's room and ran in, slamming the door and locking it behind me just in time. I stood with my back against the door for only a second. The door buckled and claws came through the door right beside my head. I screamed and slid under Claudia's bed. The door shook and the sounds of the animals changed. They started to howl then moan, and then they made a similar sound much like the ghost, wailing at a high pitch that made me cup my hands over my ears. "Stop it," I screamed. "Stop it! I want to go home. I don't want to die!"

Surrender

I had lost all faith in my intuition but it was telling me that I was beyond dreaming and somehow, I had crossed over to the spirit world. Would I ever be able to return to the real world? The thought of being in this place forever with Claudia stirred up self-pity and despair. Self-pity was especially useless for whom could I express this to? This was Claudia's world and it would be an insult to tell her I was unhappy to be here with her. "How am I ever going to get out of here?" I asked myself.

Lying under Claudia's bed all alone facing whatever world I was in, I wondered, "Is this my fault? Did I cause this? Could this place possibly be real in terms of the spirit world?" At least I was not alone. I was stuck here with Claudia until I figured out why I was here.

The real issue was my lack of faith that I would be OK if I let my guard down. It made me realize that I should let go of my expectations and just be a part of this experience. I should just take advantage of the chance to learn from this illusion. This was a lesson in spirit, I knew, and my soul was being tested and, like Murphy's Law, the outcome might be the opposite of what I expected, and whatever could go wrong, probably will.

The quiet helped me re-charge and process all the crazy emotions bouncing around in my head. As I pondered the possibilities of my new reality, a melody came to mind and I started humming, thinking of a song we learned in band. As it played out in my head, I started making up lyrics.

I'm growing on a broken heart
Where did all the madness start
Growing on a broken heart
Where did all this madness start
And with this broken heart
I'll make a brand new start.

I kept humming along, wallowing in my self-pity while at the same time, I was having a pep talk with myself. It helped me relax just enough and then suddenly it came to me! I realized that the only time I had seen the 'real' Claudia was when I was asleep or knocked out. My gut told me that I must go back to sleep to see her again. In a trance, in a dream within a dream, I was free to let it all unfold, later to be picked up, sorted and analyzed on some fundamental level once revived. I had lost the song rising out of my pseudo-physical world into dreamland where nothing is perfect, organized or structured but random and flowing....like a stream that flows through a valley. Faith was my raft and I was drifting on the cool waters, just humming my song, watching the sun ripple their surface with stipes of gold.

The Waking Dream

"What on earth are you doing under my bed?" Claudia asked. I had fallen asleep to a song I had made up and that in itself was enough for me to chuckle. Even funnier was my perspective. Lying on my belly with arms crossed, I raised my head, opened my eyes and looked up from under the bed almost ramming my nose into her forehead. She was lying on top of the bed stretched to the edge, hanging over it, her hair reaching towards the floor. It should have shocked me — a girl scared stiff, hair standing straight up — but I knew it was the real Claudia and she was upside down.

"My dear boy, why would you hide under my bed unless we are playing a game? Do you want to play a game?" she asked, a gleam of excitement in her eyes. She slid off the bed and laid beside me on the floor.

"Sure" I said. "If you can't beat 'em, join 'em," I thought, proud of myself for not being startled by her surprise introduction. This is going to be fun, I thought, letting the reality of the situation flow right past me. Just then another melody came into my head like that of a scary movie with the creepy violins and deep bass. The thought of hanging out with a dead girl tugged at my conscious and a chill ran down my spine, but the feeling could not turn me.

I chuckled out loud.

"What is so funny?" she asked.

"Nothing, I am just happy to see you again," I said. "Let's play." The scene had changed back to a semi-normal state. The room turned friendly and familiar, nothing like the cold desolation that seeped in when the ghost appeared.

"Let's play hide and seek," she offered.

"Sure Claudia, but I do not know this part of the house and I may get lost. You have the advantage," I stated.

"You should not worry about that. I will hide first and will not go far. If you cannot find me after a short time, I will give you clues so as to guide you in the right direction. I know you, Master Andy. You are a quick study."

"You don't know me at all," I retorted. "We just met."

"Yes, but my instinct tells me you are one of the sharper pencils in the teacher's desk."

I laughed out loud at her humor and it felt good. I felt like a normal kid again and was ready to let go and live a little, in her world.

"Alright, here I go!" she said. "Here is a hint: Stay to the right. This is the staffs' quarters of the house and we will stay in this part of the house. I bet you can't find me!" She jumped off the bed and ran straight to the door then paused. "Master Andy, I will show you how fun this house can be!" she said. And then she was gone.

I started counting down from ten.

I really liked this girl. She was pretty and her brown hair danced above her shoulders cheerfully.

Claudia had a smile that would light up any room and her proper speech, betraying that of an English scholar, was amusing. When I was with her, I was no longer in my self-centered, driven, always critical mode. I wanted to listen and learn from her. I have found that every time I do this, listen and let others lead, I have the most fun. There are so many ways of looking at the world and I had forgotten that mine isn't always the right way. It is so easy to take this for granted until you are bound to circumstances beyond your control. I dared myself to relinquish the wheel for awhile. I was perfectly fine with this for the moment. Claudia was driving and I was along for the ride. I ran out the door, not quite forgetting what was behind me the last time I ran in, but that thought did not slow me down. Oddly, I felt safe with her.

"Ready or not, here I come," I said as I ran out the door with a smile on my face.

Claudia's Story

To really live, you have to let go sometimes. The best way to let go is trust in others. True sharing requires nothing as you always know you can take the wheel of your own destiny anytime you like and just drive.

Somehow I knew it was my destiny to be here with Claudia. Where I was going didn't matter now. All that mattered was sharing the moment with her. Could this be my first love? I had mixed emotions but mostly desire. Time was no longer a factor and neither was space. I no longer worried about where I was and felt at peace. We were consumed by the moment. This must be what "they" call love.

As I proceeded out the door into unknown territory, I felt free. Claudia would not leave me now, I believed. We needed each other and that trust was reassurance enough to cast fear aside. I walked into the hallway and bravely took a right, not heading back towards the main entrance where the ghost, lions and gargoyles came from. I wasn't yet ready to face that again. The hallway was no longer dimly lit. I could see all the details on the walls, what little there was to see. Much of this part of the house was uninteresting and dull like a normal house. Ahead of me was the door that led to the kitchen.

I somehow knew I had been here before, but everything seemed so altered that I wasn't sure anymore. I walked slowly and carefree while listening intently for Claudia to accidentally make a sound and give her position away. The kitchen was long and there were ancient appliances there. Instead of a Maytag washer, there was a wash basin and it had what looked like rolling pins at the top. "Wow," I thought. "They didn't have electricity back then." Then I recalled the light switches on the wall. That made no sense. Did the staff wash everything by hand? Maybe it was just stored there, I concluded. The counter tops had painted white metal with a lip around the edge. The cabinet doors below were metal as well. "This would be a perfect place to hide," I thought.

I started whistling ever so softly to some rock song I couldn't recall the name of. Every memory of my real world was so vague. Besides I never was great at recalling facts, figures or especially names. But I never forgot a face, especially Claudia's dark half. The thought of her dark side gave me a chill and I could have sworn the lights flickered and dimmed as I recalled the ghastly image of her ghost. I kept whistling the song as I slowly walked along the kitchen counter sliding my hand along its surface. Tiles painted with really cheesy looking flowers and vines covered the wall behind the sink. These furnishing must have been from the early 1900's. Having no concept of history or antiques, the place looked ancient to me. An old radio sat at the end of the counter. It had two knobs and a dial like a metronome.

"Things have really changed since then," I thought. We have Pac-Man, laser tag, and go-carts.

I wondered if they even had televisions back then. I had so many questions for Claudia and pondered if we would ever be able to talk about these things, her being a ghost from the past and all. As I moved along the counter, I heard a stifled giggle. I paused, looked back along the counter and saw one of the doors under the sink slightly ajar. I turned slowly, waiting for her to do something as I knew she was dying to jump out and surprise me. I was prepared for her but I played dumb. I pretended that I heard a sound coming from the pantry across the kitchen instead.

"Come out, come out wherever you are," I teased. I was just about to open the pantry door when Claudia burst out from under the sink with a loud Boo! "Here I am. I thought I would save you the trouble as you were going in the wrong direction, Master Andy," she said. I wanted her to feel good so I didn't argue that I knew her spot. "I never thought of looking there," I said instead, flattering her. I felt as if I was treating her the same way I did my baby sister, Becca.

After a moment I went straight to the task of getting information. I had to know her story and needed to start somewhere. "Claudia, why do you call me Master, and what is it with your accent? Are you from England?"

I was never good at using psychology to get information. I probably would never be a good salesman. It took too many questions. The questions I wanted to ask, I was afraid of the answers, but had to know. A good salesperson has to ask questions to ultimately lead to answers to the real questions. "Why are you a ghost?" was my real question. To avoid unleashing Claudia's dark side I would have to ask the easy questions first.

"My parents are from Leeds, England," she said. "As for why I call you Master Andy, my parents taught me that it is polite and respectful to say Master or Madame or Miss. Does that worry you?"

"No, not at all. I actually like it," I said. She smiled at me and I smiled back. Our eyes met and I had that tingling feeling again. It was like seeing a rainbow, or knowing you had a snow day and didn't have to go to school. It was like…..Christmas. I had never felt this for a girl. It was pure joy. It was love! We paused for what seemed like minutes, the silence long and penetrating. Time had stopped and I was floating. After another moment though, it became awkward and I broke the silence. "So how old are you Claudia? I am 13," I said.

"I am 12," she stated with some reluctance." I was born in 1939 right here in this house. My parents are Leah and Harold Borne. They came here immediately after the owner, Napoleon Powell became sick. Back in 1908, Master Powell had family in Leeds who came here to help build this fabulous house. The bricks come from England as well as much of the ornamental carvings and stained glass windows.

"Have you seen the wonderful woodwork throughout? I fancy the carvings of the baby faces. They are called cherubs."

"They lend such elegance to the place! Don't you think? After the house was built, my parents came here as staff. My mother is the maid and cook. My father is the butler and groundskeeper."

At this point I had asked all the questions I needed to ask in order to confirm that she was not of this time period. I liked my science fiction and had never really believed in ghosts, time travel or other worlds. I had dared not disbelieve in God either. I usually left the unknowns at a 'maybe' but now, there was no maybe. Claudia must be a spirit trapped in this house. She had not passed on. This explanation was much easier to believe than time travel. If this was a quantum leap then where were the other people? She acted as if they were gone briefly and not forever. Did she really think they would return soon? This must be part of Claudia's denial. I was hesitant to ask, but I had to get more details. When would be the right time to ask? There is no better time than now, my impatient nature insisted.

"So," I paused, looking around as if to make the next question seem less serious, "Where are your parents now?" I knew the question was blunt. I was never good with tact no matter how hard I tried and this time I was trying to restrain myself from directly asking her the one ultimate question.

"Oh, they have stepped out to the market and should return soon. Master Andy, do you want to play more hide and seek? Would you like me to show you some special places in the house? There are many secret passageways here you know. I know them all. There are shortcuts for the staff as well." Obviously she was dodging the question, being repetitive, and wanted to change the subject. She smiled at me again and my heart made a strange flutter that was not an actual sound but more of a feeling. That feeling was immediately replaced by dread and fear as I recalled the maze I fell into in the closet. I tried to suppress it but was not so clever at hiding my emotions. Claudia sensed this and her warmth became something else and I didn't like it.

"What is it Master Andy? Are you frightened? Don't you trust me?" She paused and the tension in the room increased. The air got cold and her eyes changed again. I did not want to revisit that situation so I shook off the fear and responded quickly in an effort to rid us of the bad air.

"Of course I am not scared. I trust you Claudia. We trust each other and no one can change that, as long as we are honest with each other. I like you very much. I am game! Show me the way."

She instantly came back to life and the room did as well. There was much energy here and she was the source. I dared not pry deeper, for now. She reached out and took my hand. It was cold. I had no intentions of commenting. She looked at me with endearment and said, "Follow me. This is going to be quite exciting!"She led me to the pantry, opened the tall doors and stepped in pulling me firmly.

There were canned goods, mason jars of vegetables, bags of flour, rice and other household goods. As she led me to the left corner I thought to myself, "Maybe I have traveled into the past. Maybe there is a parallel universe in this house and I've crossed over." I dismissed the idea, thinking "I have seen too many science-fiction movies." She pushed on the side wall panel and it squeaked open.

"Wait," she said. "We need a light." She reached up on a shelf and found a match and a candle which she lit. "Master Andy, we shall go to the grand dining room from here. Hold my hand as it is dark. I do not need a light myself, as I have used this passageway many times. I want you to see, at least until you trust me. Are you still frightened?"

"No," I declared proudly, thinking of what I had already been through. I hoped it could get no worse.

"Let's go! This is fun! It's almost like being in a haunted house." Claudia turned and looked at me in a way I could not describe. There were so many emotions in her face I could not discern them all. I believe that is when she knew that I had an idea of her situation.

She lightened up, half-smiled and said, "This is going to be jolly indeed! No need to be afraid. I will protect you."

"And I, you, Miss Claudia." She was so flattered by my flirting that she actually blushed. I didn't realize ghosts could do that.

She pulled me through the trap door and into the

corridor behind the walls. It felt and looked the same as before; the light beaming through the slats made a slight glow in the tunnel but not enough to see. We moved along the way dodging cobwebs, trying not to breathe the dust we were stirring up as we went. As I held her hand and we moved along the secret inner linings of the house, I felt safe and secure, despite the fact that this world was not my own and I had no foothold in this reality.

Mother's Touch

Just the touch of Claudia's hand gave me security despite the coolness and translucency that constantly reminded me I was holding the hand of a dead person. It was, however, not even close to the security of my mother's touch, calming words and lullabies. This lack of warmth made me miss my mother and brought me back to the mornings when she would call us to the breakfast table or when she would comfort me when I awoke from a bad dream. As I reflected on her nurturing, I could hear her voice. It was more than a memory. I could actually hear her voice. "Please come back to me my darling son," she whispered. It was as if I was tucked away in my own bed and just drifting back to sleep while she was telling me a story. I heard her voice again, "I miss you Andy and I love you. You are my world." It sounded so real, echoing in my mind as if she was right there with me. There was no better security than a mother's love. Just then I heard a growl, but told myself it was only my belly.

"My parents used this passageway when they wanted to remain unseen and get to places faster," said Claudia. "Some of the guests who visited this family were not very nice to us. If we were out of sight, we were out of mind, as Americans often say." As we walked along the dark tunnel, her hand tightened on mine. She pulled me closer before turning to face me.

"Are you frightened, Master Andy?" she asked again. "I would never let anything happen to you. You are my friend. Are you enjoying playing with me?" she asked sincerely, as if the wrong answer would crush her. I was not very good at discerning if someone was just the saying words or really feeling it. I was much better at analyzing things than people. People could be so supportive and seem sincere but in time you would discover their true motives. But, I sensed Claudia had no hidden agenda only a need for my companionship. I trusted her even though I deducted that she did not want to be alone here and she wanted me to take a liking to the place so I would be inclined to stay with her.....forever. I wondered if she was permanently trapped between worlds. If so, would I be able to help her? Would I ever be able to leave?

I was not willing to give up my world entirely, but I must admit the thrill of adventure was alive again and I couldn't wait to learn the rest of the house's secrets.

The passageway ahead narrowed and veered left where I could now see the outline of a door. This must be our destination. The light around the edge of the door glowed deep red. "The grand dining room is through here," Claudia said. "This passage was designed as a way for servants to get back and forth to the kitchen while avoiding guests who gathered in the entrance off the main hallway. My mother could get things on the table quickly." I tried to imagine a maid rushing down this dark tunnel with a huge turkey and it reminded me of a song on the radio, something about cold turkeys, but I couldn't for the life of me recall the words. But I could hear the refrain in my head clearly like it was playing from another room. Tunes always popped into my head at the strangest times. There was a song for every occasion, I thought with a chuckle, even when you are in a haunted house and traveling down secret passageway with a ghost.

"What is so amusing, Andy?" she asked. I didn't reply as I knew she would not have heard the song anyway.

"Watch your step here," she said. "There is a bit of a ledge." She pushed on the door to reveal a long heavy curtain. Like the ones in the main entrance, it was made of the same thick velvety material and stretched to the ceiling.

I helped her push the heavy curtain to the side and we made our way into a huge dining area. The table was very long, able to seat at least 30 people. There were huge candelabras on the table, one on each end and the centerpiece was amazing yet eerie. Made of gold or another precious metal, it shined bright as if freshly polished. It had an eagle at the top, while various leaves, branches and snakes were intertwined around the base. As I took in the sights of the room, I felt as if I was in a castle, not just up the street from my home. More cherubs decorated the ceiling but they appeared to be made of gold. In fact, the room itself seemed to have a golden glow. Chairs with intricate carvings lined the walls and in the corner was a grand piano.

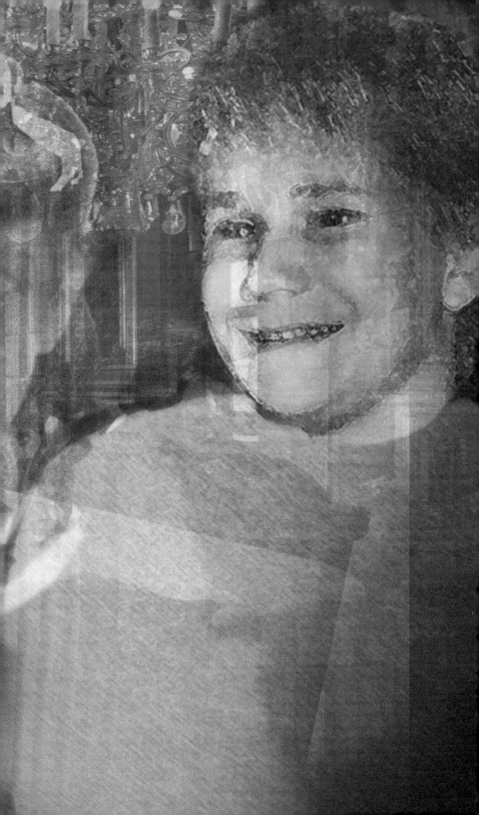

"This family must have really been fond of music," I said. "I found a special treasure upstairs, Claudia, and we should go find it when we're done here. It is a beautiful silver-plated saxophone and I was told it will be mine one day."

"Why you must be talking of Master Powell's instruments. He likes to serenade the guests while Mrs. Powell plays the piano. They sound divine together," she said.

She had let go of my hand and moved to the table where she took a seat at one end. I understood what she intended and walked to the other end and took a seat as well.

"Tonight," she claimed in a regal voice, "We will be serving roast pheasant with a honey cranberry glaze, candied carrots and a chilled salad with tomato aspic." She must have been in the presence of royalty at some point as she acted and looked like a princess from where I sat.

"Please pass the potatoes, m'Lady," I said in my best English accent making Claudia giggle hysterically. It was uplifting to see her in such good humor. I could tell she had not had much time to be a child and had suffered from some major tragedy to find herself here all alone. She had striking features. Her eyes had dark circles under them which I attributed to lack of sunshine. She was petite and had an attractive face. Her lips were tight and she had a cute chin, but when she laughed she blossomed and I could not help but stare. I wanted to kiss her. As quickly as I conceived that thought, it was tainted by the fact that I had seen her as a skeleton.

Claudia must have sensed this and her demeanor changed ever so slightly. "Do you think I am pretty Master Andy?" Before I could respond I could have sworn that the serpents in the centerpiece moved. This alarmed me to the point that I stood up and walked from the table toward her, my eyes to the floor not wanting to give her any wrong ideas. She read my thoughts. It had happened before in the kitchen. Every time I thought of leaving or of her spiritual condition, I could see the ghost inside her, the bad side coming forth. It was the side of her where bad thoughts, memories and even anger lived. We all have a dark side but hers manifested not only in her physical presence but in her spiritual form as well. I looked above me, expecting to see the gargoyles come to life and fly down to attack me like before but there were none.

Surprised by my ability to control my emotions and being much more aware of how to deal with Claudia, I responded like a boy who had already known love but was careful not to upset her. "You are a lovely girl Claudia. I like you a lot. I bet you already have a boyfriend, though."

Her eyes seem to lose their glow, she bowed her head and a look of extreme sorrow flashed across her face. "I did, but it seems so long ago. He had to leave me and move from here. Promise you will never leave me Andy. We can have so much fun together." I avoided the request but wanted to know more. "I bet you have a best friend don't you. A girlfriend to play with your dolls and drink tea together," I asked.

Her look of sadness and loneliness did not dissipate, but she looked up at me and said with a melancholy smile, "I did indeed. Her name was Sarah, but she had to move away as well. She lived here. In fact you remind me of her. We played hide and seek in the passageways when her parents were gone. We would sit in her room and have tea parties with our dolls. I miss her. She was indeed my best friend and we shared all our deepest thoughts and secrets."

I knew she was talking of my mother. It was in her bedroom where I saw Claudia's dark half and was given the runaround in the closet. I still had the letter and the key in my pocket. So, it was true that my mother had met Claudia's spirit and was inspired to write about ghosts. I could not wait to ask her about Claudia when I got home.

"We had many grand times and we trusted one another. Master Andy, I must warn you that this house has secrets and not all of them are good. Like every house, many memories live here, good and bad. You must be careful and not get lost as the dark side of the house may consume you and kill you. I will protect you. If you are ever lost and can't find your way, call my name and I'll be there." I had to hold back another chuckle as a song with those words started to play in my head.

"Don't worry. I will stay close by you as well. You are special to me and I want to spend time with you and share all our secrets," I told her. The lights flickered and the room started to fill with a thin fog.

"We must go now," she said. "There are guests coming for dinner and we should not be in this room. Besides, my parents will be back from the market soon to prepare dinner. I was standing near Claudia's end of the long table when I heard the 'clink' of silverware. Through the fog, I could see faint shapes of people appearing at the table. I could see at least ten ghostly images of people talking and socializing as if we weren't even in the room. They were obviously on the same metaphysical plane as Claudia. It was a ghost dinner! I was not surprised at the sight as I was already somewhat conditioned to the possibility of ghosts. It was almost, but not completely, amusing. Nevertheless, I did as instructed and followed Claudia to the dining room's main entrance.

"I have another secret to show you! Come quickly before others arrive."

"How many ghosts reside here?" I thought to myself. This was way better than "The Haunted Mansion" in Disney World except there were no cars to ride here. I could not wait to tell Steve of my adventures. Maybe he could meet Claudia too. The moment that thought came to mind, Claudia turned and it was no longer her anymore. The bad version of Claudia had returned. I wasn't as frightened as before, but needed the good Claudia back. This was getting frustrating. It was like dealing with someone with a split personality. This is not how most people are, I told myself, unconvincingly.

They don't have two faces, or do they?

Two Faces

Again, my inability to say what I feel, even with the best intentions, came out. I had learned much more about the sensitivity of this spirit; both of them. No matter what I said, it was tapping into my thoughts, reading me just like a good salesperson does by asking the right questions. Imagine how powerful a salesman could be if he could read minds. The energy of the question mark could channel thoughts, divert focus, sidestep sensitive issues or even humor a ghost. In the almighty battle of words I often chose the exclamation point: Less of a stealth device, it was more like a bomb. I let them fall from my mouth at times and almost blew myself up. The combination of questions and surprise could be effective against enemies and loved ones alike. My choice of words and how I used them was critical now as I was facing a very psychic being who could read me well.

"I have a friend named Steve who you would really like, Claudia. But he probably would not like it here. He is in a world where hope and adventure are suppressed by survival and everyday strife. He probably would not come," I said, keeping my weapons of expression hidden. Claudia came back instantly as if an internal vacuum had pulled the wicked, tormented and angry part of her back inside her aching soul.

The fiery glow was gone from her eyes as quickly as it had appeared. I had successfully humored the beast. I had a funny feeling that the next time I might not be so lucky. Her transformation had left me in a state of nervousness that was starting to wear my patience thin. I had to find a way to reach both Claudia and her demon at the same time. I needed to create a situation where I could ask her the right questions to force her to present both sides of herself at once. Then with a single bold statement, I could finally make Claudia come out of her denial. This would be clever of me if I could pull it off. I was flirting with powers I had no control over, except words and of course the ultimate sword, kindness. That would, in the end, slay the beast and set her free.

"Claudia are you OK?" I asked showing deep concern.

"Why do you ask that?" she replied, trying to divert the question back to me.

"You looked strange just now. Did I anger you? Was it something I said?" I pressed on.

"No, not really," she said. "I have found that there are only a few people who understand me. There is a side to me that is very protective. It sometimes causes me to act irrationally. I do not mean to act this way. I suppose fear brings out my defenses."

"Why Claudia, do you not trust me? I am your friend and by now we have grown close. I promise you I would never do anything to hurt you. I promise, Miss Claudia. You are very special to me."

She managed a half smile and took my hand.

"I know this about you Master Andy and your heart is pure. But I fret that you will abandon me, and I might not be able to bear never seeing you again," she almost whispered.

"My mother told me that love lasts forever and you will never be apart if you have love. Love never dies and one day we will all reunite in heaven," I tried to comfort her.

Just then something strange happened. Claudia did not change but it appeared that she was projecting energy into the house. As with the stained glass from the basement, a wave of colors flowed through the house. Then without warning, they changed to that metallic mist that made the walls, ceiling and even the chandelier radiate some pattern of lights. It was beautiful and wicked at the same time. My use of that one word, heaven, had confused her. She had experienced fear and hope in one emotion and her dark demon had no control over her. I tightened my grip on her hand and dared not mention the light display projected from her into the room. I had found my way to approach her but had to wait for the right moment. That is when I realized I could be a good salesman but only had to develop some patience and tact, as my sidekicks.

For the first time in my life, I was not afraid while realizing I was at that crucial moment. Her next question made me aware of another word that had influenced the moment.

"Why Master Andy, did you just say you love me?" she said. I was the one blushing now. I managed to push back a lump in my throat from either embarrassment or sincere emotion and all I could say was, "Maybe?!"

For a moment I really wanted her to be alive. A huge smile came on her face and for a moment I saw no circles under her eyes, her hand became almost warm and she looked as if she must have when she was alive.

She was radiant. A yellow light enveloped her and she actually hovered slightly off the ground.

Enduring Pain

Claudia was a strong person. Even though I had the chance to meet this girl many years after her death, I was learning much about myself through her. I wondered if I was in her shoes how my dark side would look. I imagined that being in such a limbo state would have caused me to level the house by now, rendering it condemned or demolished, leaving me homeless. Homeless. That is not just a condition but a prison. Where would Claudia reside without this house and was the house more of a home and not just an organized assembly of wood, nails, bricks and mortar?

I had learned much in my studies thus far. I was taught the basic principles in school. In science, there were laws that everything in the universe had to abide. Energy is always transferred. It is never created or destroyed. It comes from somewhere. So when a person dies, where does their energy go? This is such a difficult theory to actually prove in everyday life … and death. When we are alive we collect and spend energy and do so in patterns so unique to each person that no two people are identical. We learn to absorb, share and even steal energy from others to maintain our own lives.

When we die does the energy just merge into the physical objects around us? Or is our energy transferred to that spiritual dimension that no one can explain but everyone wants to believe in? All I knew at this point was that I was glad I had not been such a pessimist that I had rejected anything I could not see or touch. Maybe if I was one of so little faith I may not have met Claudia.

I felt blessed, joyful for this experience. It confirmed that I was not so shallow and skeptical that I was unable to let her in. I must have something others don't have, I thought. My mother must have been the same way. That was her gift to me. I felt emotions strongly, but my passion was always like an over-filled balloon ready to burst. When everything was going OK, I was OK. But when the chips were down my mother and father had taught me to be strong. Even so, I sometimes did not behave admirably. The truth is I was just no good with pain.

For Claudia's sake now, I had to be strong. If I did not help her I could not help myself. If I said the wrong thing, we might both perish. If I rejected my feelings, I might never feel. I chose not to let my heart go at this moment, but focused on finding whatever I needed to do to make it all right for us both. I was trapped now and I could not leave if I wanted to. I could try to run, but something deep inside told me to push through. It was my willpower and I realized I could make it through tough times when called upon. I just never had the opportunity to be challenged in this way.

Before Claudia had a chance to continue her inquiry of love, I diverted the conversation. Having seen what I had so far in this Big House, the adrenaline was coursing through my veins. I wanted to know more, to understand.

I was wired for sound after seeing not just one, but a room full of ghosts. It made me marvel at the possibilities of the afterlife. It promised exponential joy. I was even more thrilled at knowing that the Big House did indeed have secret passageways! It was not just an illusion. I needed to see it all!

"Claudia, where are you taking me now?" I asked. She looked as if she was returning to her normal state (whatever normal is for a tortured ghost).

"Just wait until you see this, Master Andy. These are the real secrets of the house. I believe the architect was an eccentric. Some of the mazes within this house are easy to get lost in. It is almost as if the house itself made them. I know it sounds funny but they seem to change. Even I get lost sometimes. You just have to focus in your head where you are going and you will get there. If you start to fear you will be lost or trapped, but we'll be together. When we emerge, we'll know the secret."

I recalled being in the closet and trying to follow the path but ending up in mom's sister's room. I was curious to explore the closet passageway again. That was alright, Steve and I would try it another day. She must have read that thought again as all signs of flattery and joy had vanished and she was back to her grey, ghostly self and approaching anger again. Claudia was jealous!

I quickly changed the subject. "Claudia, you mentioned you had a friend, Sarah. Tell me more about her."

Claudia was obviously disturbed and didn't even

acknowledge my request. She quickly grabbed my hand and led me back away from the stairs toward what must be the front entrance.

"Come," she said, "I will show you the way to her room through the passageways. We played hide and seek in these tunnels. I taught her how to use them but her family did not approve when she disappeared and then popped up in odd places. I never talked to her family. I only spent time with her, as she was good, like you, Master Andy. You are special in that you are not a doubting kind of person. You see the good in things. You are not a pessimist."

Claudia either was gaining trust in me or she had just let it slip that she knew her condition, stuck between life and death, her spirit having not yet passed on. She obviously was aware then that I was alive like my mother and was not supposed to be with her forever. She was making the best of it and we were both trying hard not to state the obvious: that we would have to part sometime.

Instead, out of respect and desire to enjoy what time we had together, we were not ready to talk about our current state. We were going to have some more fun and truly explore the Big House despite our fears and loneliness, our uncertainty.

The Clock

She led me down a short hallway and into a huge room with tall ceilings, much higher than in any room I had seen thus far. I tried to recall how the Big House was when I was here last. Nothing looked familiar. Could this be another part I had not seen? As we walked, Claudia started becoming translucent as if she was going to disappear although I could still feel her cool hand in mine. Pain flashed through my head and it felt like it does when you hit the funny bone in your elbow.

In this section, the house began to take on a more regal look. I had never seen this in the house before. I wondered how I would have missed this grand part of the house in my tour with Papa Joe and my own sightseeing. There were statues of goddesses with water jugs, Roman knights in full armor with huge swords in hand and even naked figurines with missing body parts. They were starting to make me nervous as I pictured them coming alive if Claudia became angry. I decided not to speak for fear of stirring the beast within her or the house. We moved into another room where there was a sitting area to the left, like a sunroom. Although the drapes were pulled back, there was no view to the outside. I briefly wondered what time and day it was but pushed the thought out of my head lest I irritate Claudia.

To the right was a huge grandfather clock. Trimmed in gold, it stood at least 15 feet tall. Its giant pendulum swept back and forth, rhythmically keeping time. When it chimed the half hour, the sound filled the whole room. It startled me and I flinched.

"Why Master Andy, jumpy are we?" she teased.

"It caught me by surprise. Besides, the echo in here is unnerving," I said defensively.

"Are you ready?" she asked. "You are going to love this." She walked to the left of the clock and pulled me to her side. We stood, backs against the wall and she pushed on a piece of the clock's decorative trim. As she let go, the wooden piece retracted and the floor below us started to move. We were standing on a semicircle connected to the wall.

It was just like the old bookcases you see in the movies! We spun around and disappeared behind the wall effortlessly. I wondered what kind of genius had designed this. It was amazing!

On the other side, the first thing I saw was a glow from above. The light was enough to see without a candle. It was almost as if we were under a moon roof although it was not bright enough to discern how far up the ceiling went. This was not what I had expected after being led into the closet and then getting the runaround behind the walls.

There was much more space in this place behind the clock, at least two arm's lengths wide. It reminded me of the basement tunnel I had scaled to get back into the house. The only difference was the walls.

Made of wood, they were obviously part of the builder's intricate design. They weren't polished and painted as far as I could tell, but by no means were they merely the back side of a finished wall. I had seen between walls of old houses and insulation was usually everywhere, nails dangerously protruding from the back side of the wall, inviting injury. These walls were grey with an almost a mossy feel. It didn't even seem like I was in the Big House anymore.

Wherever I was now, I suddenly did not have a good feeling about this. I tightened my grip on Claudia's hand as I stood there wondering what she had in store for us; my trust in her was under scrutiny. "Here I go again," I thought. "You trust too easily in people, seeing the positive side of the coin and now this could be your last naive gesture," I told myself.

I am usually an optimist. I am a dreamer and I am often let down by the reality of life as compared to the possibilities I imagine for each and every person and event. Supposedly a combination of all the signs, Pisceans have the ability to relate to others. I had always been able to say, "I understand why they would see it that way or do that." But most times I did not factor in the selfish nature of people and their own personal needs. I only saw them as I would see myself in their shoes. Right now if I were Claudia, I would want to trap me here so I would never be alone again. It was too late for me I thought. I have already allowed her to take me here. I hoped I would be able to see daylight again.

Still there was a small motor inside me, steadily running, keeping my hope alive. Part of me was still intrigued and wanted to explore. I shook off the fear and summoned up all the blind faith I could muster. "So where to now, Miss Claudia? Let the mystery tour begin!"

"Next, we will go to Sarah's room. After that Master Andy, I will take you to your treasure. You need to collect your gift from the family. Will you play it for me?" She looked at me in admiration and I felt another surge of electricity through my body but this was not pain. I felt a strong urge to kiss her again. It was her time to prove to me she was trustworthy. Surely she could not be so cruel as to tempt me with the saxophone.

"Well, what are we waiting for? Lead the way," I insisted. She pulled my hand and drew me close behind her. My arm touched the back of her leg and I totally forgot her condition for a second. It felt like rocket fuel going through me. Having recently reaching puberty, I knew exactly what I was feeling and shut down that response as quickly as I could, for many reasons, mainly … she was a ghost. The physical and emotional confusion together made it easy to reject the arousal and I let it go. There were two paths and she went right.

"The other direction leads us to a trap door on the porch leading out of the house." she said in a tour guide manner. She was really enjoying this and I was again compelled to trust my good opinion of her. "Too late anyway," I thought.

What did I have to lose?

As we left the open area behind the clock, the light faded. Up ahead there was another open area lit from above as well. The path we followed was getting narrower with every step. We had to turn sideways to pass. The walls were cold and there was a musty smell. It didn't make sense that there was no insulation here. "How is the house able to remain warm?" I wondered.

Claudia paused for a second, her grip tightening in mine. I was imagining the saxophone and how to get to it. Then I heard what had stopped her. It was a low growl of what sounded like a lion or wolf. It was so faint I might have been able to pass it off as a squeaky board. But Claudia had paused and that gave me cause for alarm. What could possibly scare a ghost? She was already dead.

Beasts Within

There was something unsettling about the narrowing corridors. It reminded me of my initial descent into the basement tunnel. Suddenly I felt the need to get out of here, from behind these walls. I tightened my grip on Claudia's hand and bit my lip, afraid to say another word. She led us through the narrow pass and I felt more than panic. It was a sense of dread, as if this would be the end. Now, simply having the bond with Claudia and being close by her side was not enough to ward off the fear. I felt we were both in danger. Were the walls closing in? I had always been a little claustrophobic.

"Please hurry, Claudia. I think something is following us," I said in an urgent whisper. As I spoke, I heard the unmistakable sound of a heartbeat. It was so faint I almost felt it more than I heard it. She said nothing and kept moving forward, holding my hand tightly. It seemed like we would never get to the next open area. The walls were not closing in but almost swelling now. As we pushed on, we had to squeeze through as they contracted and released. It was not my imagination. The walls seemed alive and breathing.

"Don't look back Master Andy. Keep ahold of my hand. We are almost there," she whispered timidly. "Trust me, we are almost there."

The rhythmic sound was growing. It was pulsating just like a heartbeat. The walls seemed to be moving with the sound. It was like we had been swallowed by a beast and were in its belly. The sound was familiar. I recognized it, but in my state of panic I could not recall from where. Half way through the narrow path, I suddenly wanted to turn back, every fiber of my being telling me this was wrong.

"We can't make it Claudia. Let's go back," I begged.

"Don't fret, we are almost there. If we turn back now we will surely be devoured. I am sorry Andy," she said, her voice full of fear. "It must feel your presence. Don't let go of my hand. We are almost there."

The sound was getting louder and I could feel the pounding of the walls in synch with it. It wasn't a heartbeat. It was the clock, the tick-tock booming and resonating through the walls. I could see the end of the narrows up ahead. We were almost through and just in time as I felt at any moment the walls would squeeze me to death, squashing me like a grape. I could not see Claudia's face, but I knew we were in danger. She had a grip on my hand so strong that it hurt and she was breathing heavy. Just as her hand crossed into the open area and the faint light fell on it, I felt a tug from below.

Then I heard a menacing growl. It wasn't the lion; it sounded more like a demonic wolf. It growled and sunk its claws into my left leg. I screamed.

"Claudia, help! Something has me. Don't let go of me," I pleaded. I felt pain though my shoe but more so, I felt paralyzing terror. I was being pulled backward and hard!

The beasts had me and I was going to die. "Claudia!" I screamed. I felt her hand losing its grip on mine, then there was another sharp tug and she only had hold of my fingers. I knew something wasn't right when I went behind the clock. So much for instinct. At least it wasn't Claudia I was afraid of. She was not the beast.

To my horror, I realized I was being pulled back from where I had come: the basement. Barely holding on, Claudia looked past me at the beast. Her eyes glowed a fierce red. The sound was now unbearable. It was getting louder and faster, the walls contracting and expanding with each "boom." It did not want us to pass! The thought of being consumed by the house made me wish I had never come back here for my treasure. I wished I had never seen the Big House. Greed had led me here and I was afraid I would never make it back home.

In one last blast of adrenaline, I kicked the creature with everything I had. It sunk its teeth even deeper into my heel and the pain shot through my foot all the way to my head. Claudia was not the one in charge here. I suddenly realized it was the house that was trying to kill me. It must have come alive with jealousy after sensing my attraction to Claudia. She had been trapped and the house was not going to let me take her from here. We were both trapped and had to break free before it was too late. I screamed as the pain consumed me.

"Let go of him!" she bellowed, as the fiery red glow from her mouth lit up the whole tunnel. I turned just in time to see the beast that had a hold of me. It was a huge wolf-like being standing at least five feet tall. It had a long jaw and razor sharp teeth. Its hair was matted and foamy drool from its mouth dripped all over my shoe. Its claws were dug into the floor and I realized now we were in the same place as the basement tunnel, dirt below our feet. The walls had the same texture and hairy roots protruded straight out of the soil. They were twisting and growing at an alarming rate. One of the roots slithered around my waist and tried to pull me back.

As Claudia dragged me forward, I could feel the heat from her breath and it felt like rage. "Let go of him. I command you!" she yelled. Startled, the beast backed up and howled. Hair bristling, it prepared to strike again. The walls now had me tied up in the vines, squeezing the breath from me. Claudia regained her grip on my hand and tugged with all her might.

"I don't like you anymore. I don't want to be here anymore. I am tired of your games. Leave us alone!" she screamed, this time the light turning to real fire. Behind me, the wolf-like creature burst into flames, its hair singed and smoking from her blazing breath.

Claudia pulled hard on my arm and again she took a deep breath, raised her head and screamed, "You will not have this boy! And now you will not have me. Let go of him or I am gone forever!"

Suddenly, the vines loosened their grip on me and the walls stopped pulsating, and I understood, if not too late.

We fell forward and all went silent except for the steady heartbeat which was so loud that even my hair pulsated.

"Run!" she screamed. We scrambled to our feet and pushed through the slimy narrow corridor into an open area. The mad red glow was gone from her face. Just past the open area, we came to a dumbwaiter in the wall. She rushed to open the door but it was stuck. Several piercing shrieks cut through the pulsing sound of the house and clock. The ground shook and it sounded like a stampede coming our way. We tugged at the dumbwaiter door but it wouldn't budge. In desperation we pulled with all our might and the rust finally broke free.

She pushed me in, pleading, "Hurry Andy! They are still after us. Hurry!"

As I grabbed her hand, I could see several wolf-beasts tearing through the narrows, tripping and climbing over one another as they pushed to get to us. They were monstrous and dripping in ooze from the basement tunnel. The vines were encroaching on us as well, climbing toward the chamber we were in. The wolves surrounded us as I pulled Claudia in, one of them biting her leg as we frantically tried to kick them back. I yanked the rope to close the door and it would not budge. The rope was stuck, the old pulley frozen with rust, decades past any useful operation. I pulled again. Nothing happened.

"Help me pull!" I yelled to Claudia. She grabbed the rope and we yanked on it while I was kicking back the jowls of the beasts, their snarls and howls now louder than the heartbeat of the house. We tugged together and the door slammed shut. The beasts howled in anger and pain as the door closed over their mouths. but were clawing into the siding of the pullcart.

"Pull the rope, Andy. It will hoist us upstairs. Pull hard!" There was some resistance and I could see the vines encircle the box we were in, wriggling between the cracks of the door. "Pull harder!" she screamed in desperation.

We could not get free. We tugged as hard as we could but the roots had wrapped around the dumbwaiter. You could hear the beasts growling around us, biting and scraping the exterior. They were so strong that the enclosure started to give.

"We are going to be crushed!" I exclaimed. I looked at Claudia, her face was full of terror, panic and still there was something else; more rage. As she pulled on the rope, I saw her eyes light up again, changing in color from red to yellow to bright white as the light grew in intensity. Then she let out this high-pitched wail. The dumbwaiter shook and I was blinded by the light and my lungs filled with smoke. Immediately, the vines gave way and we were propelled up at lightning speed. The rope slipped though our hands and we slammed to a stop at our destination. Everything went quiet and we just sat in the dumbwaiter hugging each other and catching our breath, both of us afraid to open the door and step back out into the house. For a second I almost didn't notice that she felt warm and alive.

Letting Go

Trust is such a hard thing to earn and yet so easy to lose. Claudia and I had not known each other for very long but there was an immediate bond between us.

In every life there are elements that compliment and play against us every step of the way. We may live in harmony for many years in certain environments or conditions, not even aware of our true situation. It takes a different perspective to truly see what condition you are in. It is only by comparison that we can really recognize who we are and the path we are taking. The problem is that we are all somewhat in denial as to who we are. There are so many roads in life and our options are infinite. Most have not chosen their condition. It is chosen for us either by our parents, God or merely fate. We accept the reality we are in from birth and we adapt and grow or slowly die. This is the world we know. But along the way, especially as we get older, we are given many opportunities to see our reflection through the eyes of others. The validation we receive is not always welcome or even interpreted correctly. The viewpoints we get are not always as things are.

No one could describe the relationship between Claudia and I, but I am sure they would enjoy expressing their view of this world I was in now. And it did not matter. Claudia and I now had a trust that was true and unbreakable. None of us are perfect and at times we are all selfish, but to be truly selfless shows that you trust yourself and someone else enough to let go and be vulnerable on their behalf. That takes much courage and we had just proven that our faith in each other was strong. We were almost like one now, each of us forever changed and a part of each other through this experience. No one or nothing could change that, not even the Big House. For a moment, I wondered if I were in the midst of some horrific nightmare, but I decided even if that were so, I'd never forget her. Besides, I was bleeding and could still smell the wolves.

"Master Andy," she whispered and then paused. There were tears in her eyes and she was shaking as we held each other. For a moment I had forgotten her immortal status and we were one body sharing everything, every emotion. We were invincible but at this moment so vulnerable. "I am so sorry for putting you in this awful situation. You have to believe me that I would never do anything to harm you. I always knew there was an evil side to this house but I thought it was merely being protective. Now I see that it has no regard for me." She held me tighter and pleaded, "Please forgive me."

"Now Claudia," I replied. "It is not your fault. You did not do this to us. There is something more than just us in this house, much more. I am no longer scared and you should not be either. As long as we have each other, we are safe. Without complete trust and honesty, we are vulnerable to the house and it will try to defeat us."

I held her and slowly stroked her hair.

I was compelled to get out of the dumbwaiter and run to a safer place. I had no idea where we would be safe as now it appeared that the demon was the house itself and we were in it. "Claudia, there are some things I need to tell you but we need to get out of this box. Where is the safest place in this house for us?"

"Sarah's room," she announced with ultimate confidence. "This is where I always go to escape from my world. We used to hide under her bed and talk for hours. When her parents were looking for her, we were invisible. They never found us. We met there most nights. That was our safe place. I even feel that she is with me sometimes when I am afraid and all alone. I miss her terribly. She is like no other, Master Andy."

I was bursting at the seams to tell her the truth but this was not the place. I had no idea what was out there and we were both terrified to leave the box, much less each other's embrace.

"OK, we will go there, but forget the wolves, I have been chased by lions and gargoyles and they may still be out there. We will have to make a run for it. How far is it to her room from here?"

"We will come out at the end of the hall. We need to run back toward the stairs to the second door on the left," she said.

"Is there another way? Those lions were huge, much bigger than the wolves and we will not be able to outrun them."

"We can go through her sister's room then. It is the first door on the left. I never felt right there. Her sister refused to acknowledge me, and made fun of Sarah. Everyone thought Sarah was crazy because she had an imaginary friend. There may be danger in her sister's room, as well," she whispered. "But if we are quick we can make it. All we have to do is get through her room to Sarah's room. From there we will be safe under her bed."

"Let's see if the coast is clear," I warned her. "If all is quiet I will go first then you can take the lead."

"Don't worry, I am just as afraid as you. It is clear the house no longer likes me, but they cannot kill me, of course.... We are both in danger," she confided, trying to hide her gaffe.

For a moment I could see her eyes even in the pitch dark. They had that familiar green, loving glow. Her hand clenched around mine and she moved her face close and I felt like I might faint.

"Andy, in case something happens to either of us, may I be so forward to ask you for a kiss,...... for good luck?" she asked coyly, as if I would reject her.

Before I had the chance to respond she kissed me. I had never been kissed before, besides my mom, and it was heaven.

FORREST
LEE

SGT
19 AAF BASE UNIT
WORLD WAR II
JANUARY 7 1990
JUNE 20 1943

LAUDIA

The Confession

I was experiencing so many emotions by now, I felt like my body was humming; vibrating at random frequencies. I could not control my mind. It was like watching a car wreck right before my eyes. My brain was processing everything as fast as it could but there was some lag time. I was in shock, in love and ready to implode from the claustrophobia. I could not see her face but I could see and feel her aura and it was warm and embracing. My first priority was to get out of that box. Romance could wait.

I paused after the kiss and stuttered, "uh,… how is your leg? Did that thing bite you?" I was not very happy with my response. For a second I had forgotten that she was not of the same physical plane. Her kiss felt so real and wet and warm. "Is that the only thing you can say after a first kiss? Dork!" I thought.

"It's not a worry, Master Andy. Are you in pain?"

"I'm OK," I quickly replied. "It bit my leg but I can walk,…. I mean, almost run." I could hear the awkwardness and panic in my voice. "We have to get out of here Claudia. Make sure I go the right way. Ready?"

"Yes, Master Andy," she said in an even softer tone. "I am not afraid. I am with you."

"And, uh, Claudia …I love you." There I said it and it felt good.

"Here we go. Please God be with us," I said.

"I love you too, Andy," she added. Her hand in mine was warm and real. She smelled of Nini's roses.

I opened the door ever so quietly but to no avail. It squeaked and the echo filled the hallway. I peeked out and saw no movement. I trained my ear on the opening and heard nothing. We were at the end of the hall and I could see the top of the stairs far at the other end, one lion's head at the top of the rail. The house seemed back to normal. I took a deep breath and stepped down into the hallway.

It was amazing how different Claudia looked now. Was she actually coming back to life physically or was it my wishful thinking? She was less pale and more beautiful than ever, almost radiant. It was nothing like her episodes when she was glowing with rage. She looked healthy, beautiful, normal. She had the look of love.

As I helped her out of the dumbwaiter, I staggered and her body fell into mine, both of us barely braced against falling. We froze for a second and stared into each other's eyes, blushing. We kissed quickly once more.

From the carved wood on the stair railing, we heard a loud crack. The lion was coming alive. The sound of splintering wood was followed by a roar that shook the floor beneath us. As the claws from its huge front limbs emerged, we were off and running at full speed, the door only a few yards away. It was the most intense distance I had traversed in my life.

Out of the corner of my eye, I caught the glow from a gargoyle's eyes as it was flying straight for me, swooping in from the side. It shrieked and flew toward my head, grazing my ear with its talons, reinjuring my headwound. The wind from it was cold and smelled like a mixture of metal and blood. I ducked just in time as we closed the door on the flying thing. We could hear it bounce and slide off the wall squawking in anger. Then silence. We were in. I was so terrified I forgot where we were and ran straight for the bed.

"No Master Andy, silly boy, we must go to Sarah's room. She cast a spell there that will keep the house from harming us," she reminded me. I had forgotten that both rooms were almost identical. We ran through the adjoining door and slid under the bed. Had this door been there before? I didn't let the question linger in my mind. At this point we were finally in a safe place: a place for Claudia to call home. That word 'home' rang in my head as I caught my breath under the bed holding Claudia's hand, both of us staring at each other with slightly uneasy grins. After a short pause, our eyes never wavering, I kissed her again. No matter how tender the moment, I could not get the thought of home to leave my head. Despite my longing for home, I wanted to stay in this moment forever, embraced in her love. I wanted to be both places at once.

Although I dreaded it, the moment had finally come when I felt a certain obligation to set the record straight, not so much for me but for Claudia. Maybe by helping Claudia admit to me she was no longer among the living would help her to be free from the prison we called The Big House. Maybe, in the grand scheme of things, I was here to help her move on. I would never know until I tried. Knowing there were powers that were against me, I was still reluctant. I could be making things worse but I owed it to Claudia to try. And I owed it to myself as well. I knew now that I was not the only one being held prisoner in this house.

"The truth will set you free," I thought. I found some humor in this. My Nini always told me that the simplest and oldest of rules always apply. So I used her advice and decided to just say it. I was really exhausted but still slightly hopeful that this simple quote would hold true.

"Claudia, I need to tell you something," I said with some reluctance. As I spoke, I could hear stirring outside my mother's bedroom. There were moans and shrieks but they seemed muffled and far-off. It must be the house frustrated by my attempt to set Claudia straight. I wondered if the house would come down around us if I continued to reveal the truth. I was afraid but had to take a chance.

"Yes Master Andy," she replied.

"First, I need you to promise me that you will not get angry. I want you to know that you can trust me and that I would never do or say anything to hurt you."

"Yes Master Andy," she replied again. "I trust you and I feel the same. What is it?"

This was going to be difficult. In situations where I had the opportunity to lie or tell the truth, it never failed that when I took the easy way out, I lost. When I mustered the courage to say the truth, the actual moment of confession was painful but immediately followed by relief. Like having a heavy load on my back, it was immediately gratifying to relieve myself of the burden by telling the truth, even if the initial moment of fear and doubt was so hard to stand up to. The right thing was never the easiest thing to do, but in the end it was all for the best. I knew this was one of those moments and the first words would be hard to spit out. I hoped the worst would be over if I just stepped up to the plate.

"Claudia, I need to tell you some things. It is not going to be easy for you to understand but I need some answers as well. I don't know why I am here but I believe with all my heart that I am here to help you."

"Help me, Master Andy? Why, I am fine!"
Here was my moment and I had to start somewhere. I decided to start softly.

"Claudia you may find this hard to believe, but Sarah is not only your friend, she is my mother. We live not far from here. She used to live in this house when she was a girl."

I braced myself for what could happen next and looked in her eyes expecting them to light up, or her bad side to come out. All I heard was more noise from outside the room and I jumped when there was a bang on the door. The house was furious by now, but Claudia was calm...for now. "I must get this off my chest before the door opens and I am pulled away from the safety of this spot," I thought.

"I know Master Andy. That is why we can be together. Sarah had a gift to be able to see spirits, at least mine. You must have the same gift."

"Why are you here Claudia?" I asked despite my fear of how she would respond. There was a moment of silence and her eyes turned down, staring at the floor. Then she squeezed my hand and looked back at me.

"My parents are dead and I am too, Master Andy. I have been this way for so long, I almost feel as if it never happened. I became sick with a dreadful illness. My mother and father were terribly worried. I had a fever and my mother put me in the sink with ice water to get the fever to break. My mother did the best she could. She informed the Powells and they summoned a doctor and left the house. By the time the doctor found out it was malaria, it was too late. My poor father was terribly upset. The last thing I recall is my parents arguing. I heard my father telling my mother if she had called the doctor earlier, there may have been a chance to cure me, though he didn't think I was well enough to hear them talking. Mother started to weep uncontrollably and it made my father angrier. They were standing at the kitchen door which led down the stairs to the backyard. I was lying on a makeshift bed in the kitchen, so weak I could barely move.

They didn't know I was conscious enough to hear them. He grabbed her and shook her, telling her to get a hold of herself. She tried to break free and fell backwards, down the steps. She collapsed at the foot of the stairs and my father ran to her, screaming and crying. She had broken her neck and died instantly. He cried out for help but no one heard him. All of the other occupants of the house and the servants had already left when they had learned that malaria had struck."

I did not know what to say. These moments made me go blank and I found it hard to express myself. All I could say was, "That is terrible, Claudia. Did anyone show up to help?"

"Everyone was afraid they would catch the disease and so they had quarantined us while trying to find a cure. The doctor was to return that afternoon. When my father picked my mother up from the yard, I could see blood trickling down the side of her face. It was terrible, Master Andy. I saw him bring my mother inside and lay her on the floor. He was hysterical and kept trying to revive her. Imagine how he was feeling, Andy. Here was his beloved wife dead on the floor and his daughter suffering terribly from the fevers of malaria. It happened so quickly."

"Why didn't he run for help? Was there no one who could come? Where was the doctor?" I asked, the male part of my mind looking for a solution to the problem, unable to accept the harsh reality of the situation.

"The entire town was fearful of infection. My father

didn't want to leave either of us and no one would come to our rescue. I had never seen my father cry before but I remember he was slumped over her body crying and pleading with God to help us and forgive him. As I lost consciousness I remember hearing a loud bang like an explosion."

I could not speak, tears welling up in my eyes. My grip on her hand was so tight she yelped, signaling me to loosen up. I could not hold back the tears. I felt all the pain that she had held inside all these years and it rushed into me like a tsunami. She wept with me and we held each other in silence. Moments passed and my sobs subsided. I stroked her hair and looked in her eyes. "That is the worst tragedy I have ever heard. "What happened to you? Did no one come to save you?" I asked, my heart torn between rage and anguish.

"No Master Andy. By the time someone came it was too late. My father must have seen me lying there not moving and could not deal with the thought of losing us both. After the gunshot, I awoke for a few minutes and could see them both lying dead on the floor. Shortly after that I drifted into a coma and died, my spirit stuck in this house."

"Someone did come to save me though, eventually. It was you Master Andy. You are my savior. I am at peace now. But you must go. You see, Master Andy. Although my life ended long ago, time is of no measure here."

"My God, Claudia, that is a really tragic story. It is such an unfortunate thing to happen to such a wonderful person."

"Master Andy, I have been this way for so long now, I am no longer angry, sad or even in despair. I had become a friend to loneliness. But I was sent a gift from God and it was in the form of a handsome young boy," Claudia said.

She took my hand. "It is like waking from a dream only to drift back to sleep. But I am afraid that I will be trapped here for eternity, all the memories of the house twisted into the fabric of my soul. The house will insist on keeping us here so we must plan your escape."

"Our escape!" I insisted. "The only weapon we have is each other. Your love will save me. But I can save you as well, Claudia."

She said softly, " I don't think you realize how you got here do you, Master Andy?"

"I don't really recall. It's fuzzy. Everything has happened so fast," I replied.

It was true what Claudia had said; time was not a factor anymore. How long had I been here? How did I get here? I suddenly realized that I had had no reference of time since the house swallowed me up into the basement below. Every time I tried to recall the previous events, I was distracted by the house, my own thoughts or the pain in my head.

"Andy, you are in a coma. That is why we are together. Your body is still alive but your spirit is in limbo stuck between worlds. The spiritual world has opened its arms to you but you are not ready yet. I am ready to move on and have been for some time," she said. Just then I felt my heart break.

Claudia was my first love and we could never be together. Life wasn't fair. At that moment I knew I would never forget her; our souls were entwined forever.

My mind must have sensed my heart's pain and it kicked in to protect me. I tried again to recall the course of events that led me here and it was no coincidence that I felt an electric shock. Starting in my head, it ran through my body and I fully expected bolts of electricity to shoot from my limbs, but nothing of the sort happened. My eyes were closed but I could feel the Hopkins Boys on my trail, could hear the whizzing sound like an insect of the rock approaching my head, could taste the blood as the rock made impact on my skull, and the throbbing pain that was now so evident.

So this is what it is like being in a coma. Memories of events are gone, but memories of places and people remain hard-coded into the soul. Space and time no longer exist as they do in the physical world. In the spiritual realm, only emotion triggers memories. There was not a real-time connection between these places, and I surrendered my efforts to recall what happened, why I was here and when it occurred. The only tangible concept my mind could manage to deal with was the present where there was only chaos and fear.

I was stuck here.

Finally, I was able to truly be honest. Claudia was saving me! I started to cry again, and this time, she was the strong one.

Just as in life when we struggle through the battles in our heads, letting our hearts guide us, love triumphs leaving us fulfilled and justified. It made me think of all the poor lonely people tortured daily by the denial of the most basic elements: love and family.

Claudia said to me, very calmly, "I have been blessed and now I am ready to move on. Now all we need to do is convince the house to let you go. It has a soul too, you know. All the emotions that were shared in this house by the people that have been here are forever etched in the woodwork and fixtures. In this realm, it is as much alive as you and I."

Intuition

As we laid there under the bed I could still feel the frustration emanating from the house. I could sense the tremendous power that was all around us, cornering us. Although unnerved, I was relieved that now I had an ally, Miss Claudia. We were walking on thin ice and I had that feeling of swimming upstream again. I hated feeling vulnerable.

Oh the silly games we play when dealing with sensitive people and now in this case, a house! I did not want to play these games anymore and was not quite ready to face the house again. After going through mental gymnastics to humor Claudia, I was in no mood to do it again. Claudia knew all along that she was a ghost and that I was in a coma! Why couldn't we have just cut to the chase, avoiding all the frustration? But perhaps otherwise, the outcome might be fatal.

Trapped with Claudia under mother's bed, I suddenly realized I had my mother's intuition. She could get along with anyone and she was a better person for it. She was content to just be herself and had the ability to be sensitive to other's feelings, knowing that her strength was not in competition but in sharing. Her karma was extremely powerful. She always seemed to understand how people felt. She was always there to lend a sympathetic ear and she had a knack for saying just the right thing without patronizing people. Unlike her, I was more of a talker than a listener.

We had been hiding for what seemed a very long time now and I was starting to get annoyed. Part of me wanted to fight our way out of the house but the practical side of me knew better. At the same time I even felt a little sorry for the house. It didn't want to lose its sole occupant and I understood its frustration. In the end, just like anyone, it just didn't want to be alone.

Now we would have to convince the house that we were not going to leave. We were going to have to pretend. If the house was able to read my thoughts and emotions, it was going to be difficult to hide them. I trusted my sixth sense and now it told me to be very careful what kind of vibes I was emitting. For someone like me who hated to play games, this was going to be an extreme challenge.

My ability to trust my instincts gave me a boost of self-confidence. I had just successfully navigated through a wild experience and had handled the situation valiantly for the most part. It was almost funny how Claudia and I had humored each other enough to get to know each other and found we were more alike than not, both of our souls connected in this state between life and death. So, I was in a coma with a ghost and the house had us prisoner. What was to become of us?

For some reason, I felt tranquil and at peace after all my rationalizing. I didn't know and didn't care what would happen next. I only wanted to be with Claudia.

I did not want it to end but I knew that our time together was limited. If Claudia and I parted forever from this spiritual plane would I ever find love again? The thought of never seeing her again hurt me physically. The moment of salvation had come and despite our pending separation we both were happy to merely have found each other and would make the best of it!

This resolution filled me with a sort of glee and inspired me once more to face the house. I was in love which was better than any drug, money or power could yield. I felt invincible again. I felt free. I felt like singing and before I knew it I was belting out a love song based on some composition I had learned on my clarinet. The words just came before I knew what I was singing:

Here I am today
Tomorrow you go away
Tell me what should I believe
Is it part of my destiny?
Should I let go
Of my dreams of gold
Or should I still believe
That soon I'll find destiny
Is it here, has it gone
Should I turn back or carry on?

I guess I'll just have to wait and see
Where my destiny will take me.
Do you believe in destiny
Or do your realistic ways
Keep you from dreaming of better days?
Well I believe in destiny
I guess I'll just have to wait and see
Where my destiny will take me.
Oh Sweet Angel
Is your destiny here with me?

I sang to Claudia as I held her hands in mine, swinging them back in forth. After I was finished there was a long moment of awkward silence as we stared at each other lovingly.

"Master Andy, that was lovely. Did you just compose that on the quick? I am speechless."

I had nothing to say either and was amazed that I was able to conjure these words from my heart. I was emotionally exhausted, overwhelmed and that was when my best lyrics came; straight from the heart. She stared at me with starry eyes but I could tell from her expression that she was entertained by my beet red, blushing cheeks. Her loving gaze started changing into a cringe. After all we had been through my lullaby was the icing on the cake! All the stress we had bottled up for so long suddenly uncorked violently and we both burst out laughing. Once we started we could not stop.

We were decompressing from the nightmare. I felt like I would explode from the laughter, my gut aching in spasm. Claudia was howling so hard the tears were running down her face, each one sparkling as it fell with an enchanting glow; the essence of her own soul pouring out of her in joy.

As we struggled to control our hysteria, my stomach cramping from the release, I noticed the air in the room had changed and I caught a whiff of wisteria. It was such a sweet smell. The room had grown lighter. The sounds from outside the door had not dissipated, but changed to something with a melody instead of a moan. Was the house laughing with us? When we finally managed to contain ourselves, Claudia asked, "Where did that come from?"

"I don't know. I just made it up. I have this funny way about me that when I am thinking about serious things, a song will come to mind and it will describe my thoughts to a tee. It always makes me tingle inside. Music helps me make light of the harsher side of life, that, and laughing!" I said.

"That is quite wonderful. Please, when a song or a laugh comes into your head, don't hold it in. Share it and don't worry about being embarrassed if it makes you feel better. I wish we had more time to talk but I am afraid that we could be in serious trouble as the house seems to be somewhat unstable. I think, Master Andy that it is also afraid of being alone. It may not let us leave. We will have to outsmart it."

"Claudia, did you notice that when we were laughing

there was a smell of flowers in the air and the light changed?" I asked.

"Now that you mention it, I think the house was laughing along with us. It is almost like it reflected our happiness." She replied after turning to take a quick peep out from under the bed.

"The whole time I have been in the house I have felt that it has been reading me and playing on my emotions so I try not to think bad thoughts. When I am afraid, the house plays on my fears," I explained.

"So, we must be careful not to think dark thoughts and just think joyful ones. We should pretend we will be happy here forever while trying to escape."

I started humming a little jingle that my mother had sung to me as a little kid and soon Claudia was humming along with me. We just kept humming until we got tickled again and fell into another uncontrollable fit of laughter and were rolling under the bed. The lights immediately changed in the room and started to pulse and flicker. The house was definitely laughing with us.

After a few moments we had regained some control, our hands still clenching our stomachs to stop the spasms. I thought of what my Nini always said, "Laugh and the world laughs with you. Cry and you cry alone." Thinking about my grandmother made me miss home and as expected, the lights flickered again and went out.

This place was definitely in tune with my emotions. I had to be careful.

I had forgotten about the key and mother's notes and suddenly remembered them. I pulled them from my pocket. "I found these in my mother's drawer!" I exclaimed, holding out the letter and the key. "She must have written this after meeting you, but she never mentioned anything about it to me."

"When Sarah and I would talk, it was always at night and no one knew. We agreed to keep our friendship a secret. I suspect if you ask her when you get home she will remember," she said. "After the quarantine and my family tragedy, the whole town was in shock. No one came back to the house for a few years. Eventually, your grandparents moved back in the house, hoping it was just a tragic accident and not a curse. But after awhile, the rumors and gossip of the townspeople stirred their feelings. The stigma put too much pressure on the whole family and they started building the small house next door. Your mother would sneak into the house from time to time after they built their new home and together we had some wonderful adventures which brought back some good memories into the house. I guess the house absorbed all the memories and sorted them out itself. It is moody and very protective. I think in some ways it feels responsible for our deaths. At least I know it shares my pain. It wanted to protect me. It doesn't understand that I am meant to move on and that you are here to take me."

I held out my hand and showed her the key. We stared at it for a moment and then turned our stares to each other, our thoughts in line, not needing to explain. It was our passage back to where we belonged.

"I told Sarah where to find this key," Claudia said obviously reminiscing about their time together. "The last time I saw your mother, I told her we could use the key to slip away into the banquet room which was only used for very special occasions and was always locked. My parents had a key so they could decorate for parties and tend to the room. Since there was a spare, I guided Sarah to it. We agreed to meet there and play together. The first time I visited Sarah as a spirit she was scared like you, Master Andy, but after the shock wore off we would lie here every night and talk as long as her sister didn't interrupt us."

I tried to imagine having a ghost for a playmate and it was easy to visualize. My mother and I shared the same ghost friend. Cool! Of course, no one would ever believe me, and for some reason I doubted that my mother would acknowledge it.

"She knew of my condition but we never talked about it," she said. "It was not worth mentioning. We were friends. We just wanted to play and share our time and left it at that. We planned to visit this enchanted room but before we were able to meet there, she had grown up. I wonder if your mother ever thinks of me." We sat in silence for a moment, the lights slowly dimming back to grey.

"Master Andy, do you think this key could be my gateway to heaven? Maybe it was left in her drawer for you to find one day."

"Well, it's worth a try," I admitted, having no other options to consider at this point. "The key was important to her and she wanted you to go there with her. I hope you are right. I have noticed that I can't find the front door of the house. It doesn't look the same as when I came here before. It may be that the house was fooling me and trying to keep me here. This last time, I came in through the front door but ended up in a tunnel from the basement. The basement door may be our only other option."

"No," she said adamantly. "That is the wrong way to go! If the room with the key is the way to heaven, the basement door would surely be the opposite."

"OK" I agreed. "It was scary and cold and I would not want to go back down there. Then we need to get to the banquet room and try the key. We must clear our minds so the house will not know of our plans. We should pretend we are just playing and not reveal our intentions."

"What about the treasure you came here to retrieve? Do you want to fetch it first?" she asked.

"At this point I don't think it would do much good," I said. "If I am only here in spirit, then I can't take it with me anyway. It exists only in the physical world."

"Master Andy," she started to reply.

I immediately interrupted her. "Please Claudia, you don't have to call me Master, although I sort of like it."

"Sorry. It is a force of habit," she said with a smile that made me feel like flying.

"Let's just get up and pretend that we are frolicking, carefree. Maybe the house will not realize our intentions and we can draw out its good side. If we can just make it down the stairs past the creatures, we will be OK. Are you sure this key fits the doors at the bottom of the stairs?"

"I surely hope so. If it doesn't, we may find ourselves cornered and the bloody beasts will tear us to bits," she declared matter-of-factly.

I grabbed her hand and said out loud, "Claudia would you do me the honor of showing more of this beautiful old house?"

"Cheerio" she said in her adorable English accent, and we headed for the door.

Good Spirits

There was a part part of me that didn't want to leave now. In this metaphysical place, time was of no consequence and there was a mystical draw that was so illusive and far from reality that anything was possible. It was like living a dream. I was the lead character in an adventure movie, a kind of spiritual peacemaker, fighting demons and rescuing the princess. As alluring as it was, I knew my time was running out and it was possible I would die if I stayed here too long. I must do the right thing and get back, if not for me, for my family. I could picture my mother right now; me in a coma in a hospital bed and her by my side, exhausted and on guard waiting steadfast for her son to return. The thought of her agony was enough for me to throw down my selfish desires and get back to her. I did not want her to suffer. I also knew I would miss Claudia. If she was the girl I was supposed to be with, I would have to live the rest of my life missing a part of me that I could never have again. "This is the part of life we all hate," I thought. The bitter part we choke down just to taste the sweet moments, no matter how short. I had no choice but to make the best of this moment. All I would have to take back with me was sweet memories of my first true love.

"Before we head out, Claudia, we had best be prepared in our heads for how we are supposed to act," I said with authority, as if I was the director in a big psychological fantasy thriller. "Let's pretend we are in a movie and map out our roles. The house can read our thoughts. It feels what we feel and does not want to surrender its position as protector of Miss Claudia. If it senses an emotion from me that indicates that we are leaving, it will destroy me and keep you here. It may be our only chance to leave. Who knows what is behind that door. I hope it will come to us when we get there because we will be exposed in the main hallway, all the beasts close by, ready to come out and attack."

"I agree Master Andy but I am not sure I can hide the thought of missing you and never seeing you again," she said sadly. "My heart is breaking now just thinking about it."

"That is what I am talking about. We have to have our minds right. We must put on our thinking helmets for the final battle. When push comes to shove, we have to be valiant and courageous and not look back, knowing that our hearts will always be connected. We will keep this moment and place with us forever, all we have to do is remember. Memories are all we have going forward and that is OK. It will have to be."

"I am not sure I can hide that from the house. I am sure when the moment comes, my heart will give me away," she whispered. She was such a beautiful girl. As I watched her talk in agony, expressing her fears to me with so many years of pent up loneliness and isolation a tear slipped from my eye and slowly glided down the side of my face.

She noticed it and cried as well. This was good.

We both had to get it out before we set off in our final attempt to escape, our emotional armor on, wielding hope as our only defense.

"Love is the key and the key is love," I said, feeling more than ever like I was directing a movie, the passion and excitement coursing through my veins, making me feel super-euphoric and invincible. "And we have the key, Claudia!"

"You have such a way with words Andy," she said, complimenting me.

"Not me," I said humbly but kept up the dialogue, as if I was setting a stage and all the scenes to follow. "Once we leave this room, we have to hold onto one thing, Claudia: Hope. I promise that I will always have you in my heart and that I will always miss you and love you. I pray that when my time comes, I will see you again in heaven. You need to trust me now that all I say is true and my feelings will never change. That should be easy. We both know that our souls are connected."

For a moment, I recalled my grandfather; a big man but with that boyish face even as he got older. There was something about his eyes that told me he was different. He seemed to not really be there and at the same time, he was everywhere, so relaxed in life and lighthearted. One of his friends, another elderly gentleman, was visiting him one day and he and I had a chance to talk alone. He had the same mannerisms as Papa Joe. He was talking to me about perspective, but in simpler terms so I could understand. I had just come back in from doing yard work around the big house property on a very hot summer day. He had commented on the fine job I was doing. He said to me, "Son you look like you are really enjoying your work. I bet you love how it feels at the end of the day, having done something. And the money doesn't hurt either," he chuckled in an old man laugh.

"Yes sir," I said respectfully. "I am going to Mr. Kennedy's store like I always do as my reward," I said with a tone of satisfaction and confidence in my voice.

"You do that," he said and winked. "Son, I can tell you are a special young man. You work for pride and inner satisfaction. Just remember life is extraordinary, live it that way. Most people see life as arduous and take it at face value. It is much more. It's an adventure. I can tell you have an old soul. You have inherited life from many and your insight is deep. Treat life that way. Don't worry about the trivial stuff. There is so much below the surface." His name was Mr. O'Deele and he was a kind and simple man. I had never really understood what he meant until now. I felt as if I were the old wise man.

As we were preparing for this adventure that was a matter of life and death, I couldn't help but feel a bit carefree about it. All my inhibitions were gone. I was leaving it up to blind faith. My fear of death was not even a consideration although it should have been at this moment. My life was at stake and I knew it, but something about the whole experience made me realize that it was meant to be.

Claudia and I were destined to meet and whatever the future held, just knowing it had brought me here, left me anticipating the next scene, whatever it may be, no matter how it played out. Even if Claudia could not hide her heart from the Big House, it was a chance we were about to take.

"Master Andy, I understand and I have no fear," Claudia said as if reading my mind. "I have been here so long. I have had much time to realize that we are all bound together. We will always share our lives together, the energy we have together is invincible. And having shared it, we will take it with us going forward, forever blessed by knowing each other. We are forever changed by each other. I could never be as lighthearted or adventurous as you, but I can when I am with you. Thank you, Andy, for being my friend. No matter what happens I will not worry about tomorrow, only today. I won't disappoint you. I am happy to have met you and will always love you."

"Claudia, you are my soul mate and I will always love you as well," I said. "And I believe we will be together again when it is my time to leave the physical world. Our bond is too strong for us not to be together again, one day."

Without a word, we both moved slowly towards each other. Our eyes locked and our lips joined in slow motion. When they touched there were fireworks in my head and I wished the moment could last forever. I knew this would be the last time I would kiss her and would never feel like this for the rest of my life.

As we opened our eyes, the room took on a different light. Was the sun rising outside? I suddenly realized that I had not seen daylight for a long time. I could not remember how long, but I knew that feeling of newness the sun always brought to life in real time.

"Are we ready?" I asked as we laid there just holding hands, our gazes fixed on each other.

"Definitely", she replied with sparkles in her eyes where the tears had been. "Let the show begin!"

"Remember, only think about the house. It loves the attention. Flattery will get you everywhere," I reminded her.

As we slid out from the bed holding hands, I felt like a noble man, a man with a purpose. With Claudia by my side, I was filled with confidence and serenity. I was complete. I helped her to her feet and we stood there looking at the door, wondering what would happen next. When I turned to her again, I could see a comforting smile on her face too.

We were ready. She turned to me still smiling and said, "Andy you will be dandy. This old house and I are old acquaintances. It will respect me."

As she turned her glance back to the door, her smile widened, her eyes illuminated and her whole body took on only a slight translucency as I had seen before. It was her dark side and it was arming itself, ever so discreetly.

But I saw it for a brief moment. That gave me peace. I was not dealing with just any ghost.

Claudia, too, was full of power and good energy.

"Now, Master Andy, the best is yet to come. I must show you the grand ballroom. It is after all, enchanting!"

The house seemed to like that. The accents of the room came back to life and again I could see the angels in the woodwork smiling. The place took on its old prestigious self with the golden highlights gleaming from the painted trim work. "We were back in business," I thought. "Show bizness!"

The Escape

I never felt I would be good at acting. I was always afraid people could read my mind. The best bet in most unfamiliar situations is to remain calm, smile and keep your damn mouth shut. That was never easy for me. I love to express myself, sounding off to the universe just waiting for the echo to travel around the sun and back to my ear, my words always changed and reflected by the recipients of the sound. I always loved feedback. No, I always needed feedback. Then I could adjust my tune to match that of the band I was in. That was the only way I knew to blend in. But in this case, I needed to be a leader. I needed to control the situation, not just for Claudia but for us both. I must steer the conversation. This was no time to be quiet. If I did, Claudia might lose focus. Saying goodbye is never easy and everyone wants to say one last goodbye. I was sure Claudia would not be able to hold back her sentiments.

"Please tell me about the ballroom. It sounds utterly divine," I said. "Then maybe we can go and have tea in the gardens."

Claudia smiled and winked. "Why Master Andy, that sounds delightful." She giggled and held my hand tighter. "People across the continent said it was magical. It is the heart of the house. When the grand balls were being held and the music played, all was in harmony within these walls. Such wonderful imagery guests shared of it's beauty with its bountiful gardens and people dancing quite memorialize it." I was amazed at her ability to paint the picture. She was a great actress.

We were out of Sarah's bedroom just standing, sizing up the steps. The lions' heads nestled on top did not look so evil now and there was but a hint of animation in their stares. As a matter of fact, the house looked grander than I could have imagined, each crevice a shrine to perfection. I smiled at her.

"What a wonderful house! I can only imagine how awesome it must have been to live here. I could stay here forever. There is so much to see. Let's go Claudia. After the ballroom, I want to see the view from its handsome roof too," I said and winked back. I wondered how life must have been back in the day when everything was good for her, my family and everyone who came here.

As we walked toward the stairs, pretending to stroll, I noticed the top of the chandelier. It had a glow that reminded me of light penetrating a cloud, diffusing into the huge entrance. Like the rings that surround the moon on certain nights, it had a halo. "What a spectacular chandelier," I commented, keeping the chit-chat going to prevent the fear from seeping in.

"When they built the house, they had to bring it in and hang it on the huge beams in the framing before they finished the ceiling." She spoke as if she had given this tour before. I was not sure if it was true, but she was doing a great job.

I was actually enjoying it so much that I nearly forgot the impending danger ahead. "We may actually make it," I thought for a second, almost blowing our cover. I reached in my pocket and gripped the key tightly, my palm sweating. It felt hot as metal does when it absorbs heat. Then it vibrated which surprised me so much that I jerked my hand from my pocket. It was waiting for us. We were approaching destiny, walking our path to a critical crossroads.

"Did you hear that?" I asked Claudia.

"Yes, why it sounds like music. It sounds like violins! It must be coming from below," she said excitedly.

It was as if the past was gone with no memories of the fear, loneliness or any of those feelings that had been dragging along like skeletons, weighing us down. For a moment, I could have sworn that we were both dreaming of the house and just as we were imagining it, it was presenting itself. This house could be anything we envisioned it to be as long as we had no fear, only vision. There was no room for doubt and if we could remain this hopeful, we might find a side of the house neither of us had seen: Utopia! As we embraced this feeling, we were only five feet from the top of the stairs and had to make it past the lions. I quickly looked around for something to point out to keep the façade going.

"I've always admired the woodwork here, especially the angel carvings along the ceiling, and, oh my, the stately arches with such beautiful carvings. I could swear they're real!"

As I looked around the huge ceiling over the stairwell, I noticed beautiful paintings hung on every wall. I did not recognize some of the portraits but knew they must have been my ancestors. "Were they here before?" I wondered.

"The angels were hand-carved by a famous French artist. His work is known throughout Europe," she continued.

We approached the stairs and both held our gaze forward trying not to focus on the lion heads. They were not coming out of the banister and we wanted to keep it that way. We started down the stairs and I started to sing, not making any sense and not daring to look back. Claudia laughed and we started swinging our arms to my impromptu ditty.

"Master Andy, you are the most special boy I have ever known," she laughed and kept swinging her arms bobbing her head from side to side. "Don't stop singing."

I was never good at taking compliments, always wondering if people were just saying it to make me feel better. Feeling slightly embarrassed, I stopped singing. We kept up the pace, still smiling and swinging our arms as we made our way down the long staircase. So far, so good.

We had made it past the beasts.

The Key

Born under the sign of Pisces, I was destined to be a dreamer. The difficulty of dreaming is waking up and still having that desire within you. It is much like being haunted. When the sun comes up each day, it becomes more like a dreaded voice. Unless some effort is made along the way to keep working toward it, then it becomes a thorn; a skeleton in your closet. The thorn that constantly pricked at me was the desire to play that saxophone. Ever since laying eyes on it, the instrument had become my fantasy, my symbol of hope. Maybe I would be good at it. Maybe I would be legendary. Maybe I would stink. I would never know until I tried. For now the possibilities were endless; it was my chance at personal fulfillment and had I just walked right past it again. I knew if I didn't come back here I would never know but right now, coming back to this old house was the farthest thing from my mind. I just wanted to wake from this state, grab my saxophone and get back to reality. Then she squeezed my hand.

Claudia had been trapped here for so long. Her reality was this place; lost in reverie never to wake up. I supposed it was like working your whole life in a factory when all you wanted to do was be a football player. But in this reality, when you say it, think it or act on it, it happens. If it were only that simple in the real world. Maybe it was. But if that were true, why was Claudia stuck here?

Perhaps the same went for the factory workers or people unable to follow their destiny. Maybe if they imagined themselves the center of their dreams, they could wake up to a new morning. No matter where we are in life, there is always fear. Maybe fear is the only thing that keeps us prisoner in either world. Faith has been her only weapon, now rusty but ready.

"The ballroom was off limits to Sarah and her sister," Claudia said. "It was for special occasions only. The Powells had their finest parties there, and only royalty were invited to join them. That is why I showed her where to find the spare key. She desperately wanted us to sneak off together and play there, to see the silk drapes and crystal and mahogany tables that held seated the elite. We were so looking forward to that trip to the forbidden room, but it was never to be."

I tried to recall the room on my tour with Papa Joe, but nothing stood out. Most rooms were packed full of dusty boxes and furniture covered in cloth. I was thrilled by the way Claudia described it. There were so many sides to this house or this place I was in. Now that we were more in control of our environment and charged with optimism, this house could be as beautiful as we dared to imagine.

As we approached the massive ballroom doors, I pulled the key out of my pocket. It was full of energy. I could sense the magnetism coursing through my hand and the rest of my body. It was as if it was yearning to let us in.

We paused, standing at the colossal doors. They were

not the same doors as the tea room. The ceilings downstairs were much taller and so were the doors. The brass door knobs were gleaming, shining ever so brightly as if recently polished.

Claudia and I exchanged glances as I extended my hand displaying the key. It was vibrating in my hand. She said nothing, reached out and grabbed my hand, the key firmly nestled in our grasp.

"Do you feel that?" I asked.

"Yes. Could it be it is humming in anticipation?" she replied with a look of amazement. "Before we open the door, let's say a prayer."

I was surprised to hear Claudia's request. Coming from a ghost who had had so much time to stew in remorse and loneliness, it was surprising to see her with so much faith and inspiration, especially since we had no idea what would happen or if we would ever leave here.

It must be the power of this key, I thought. The future is unknown but at least we are not alone now. For her, being alone was an eternity and now she had me. I supposed that was enough for her, but as we stood with our future in front of us, she seemed to have renewed joy. We bowed our heads and clasped our hands, they key, buzzing with energy between.

"She wants to live!" I thought. This saddened me as I knew the only chance for a life would be the afterlife. Compared to what she had been through, that was far better.

Before either of us had a chance to consider or express any emotions that might unleash the demons, I said, "Would you like the honors or would you allow me?"

"By all means, Master Andy," she insisted in her mannerly British way.

"Dear Lord, thank you for allowing me to meet Claudia, bless this house and bless us in our lives and journeys. And Lord, bless my mother and let her know I am OK. Please forgive our sins. Amen."

I lifted my eyes toward the huge doors, my excitement and wonder growing stronger.

"Amen," Claudia repeated, raising her head to look straight at the doors as well. She let go of my hand as I firmly gripped the key and took aim for the keyhole.

"Wait," I said. "I have developed a little superstition since being here." I leaned down on one knee, pulling my eye to the keyhole. I moved closer and focused beyond the door. I could see nothing but light. It was like looking at a rainbow, but I could see swirls of colors dancing all around. The music was getting louder now. It mesmerized me and I lost myself, staring through the keyhole.

The feeling was so strong I forgot about everything and I only wanted to go there now. Then Claudia pulled me back from my gaze and I regained my focus. "I am glad you stopped me! I was being drawn in by a very strong force. It was exactly like the feeling I had when I was falling into the basement, but in a good way."

"Andy for a moment you were turning invisible! If I didn't pull you out of your trance you may have disappeared. It was trying to take you in there! I want to see!" she insisted. I moved aside and she knelt down beside me and put her face to the door. "Oh, my," she exclaimed. "It is like a kaleidoscope! I have never witnessed such dazzling colors."

She leaned back and placed her hand on top of mine again. As we moved the key towards the keyhole, it started to vibrate faster and began to glow as if it was turning into gold and our hands were doing the same. This was the place we we destined find! We exchanged another glance at each other, smiling and together we slid the key into the keyhole.

Paradise

Her hand was over mine as I turned the key. The energy from the key, her hand and pure adrenaline swept through me. It was the wildest feeling ever: fear, love and faith all rolled into one moment. The key turned as far as it would go and we stared back at each other.

"Ready?" I asked.

"Ready as I will ever be," she replied, her hand still in mine and our grip on the key firm and sweaty. The sound of the tumblers falling filled the foyer like drops of rain on a tin roof. There was a pause, then a creaking sound as the doors broke free and drifted open on their own. We were so stunned, the key slipped from our hands as we stepped back half a step. Bright colors blew past us and filled the room. The colors drifted into the room like rainbows floating on the wind.

We stood there frozen, our hands still entwined. Our hair blew back from our faces as a warm breeze passed. It smelled of wisteria, poppies and honeysuckle. I was struck with awe when my eyes finally adjusted to the light. There were gardens and flowers everywhere. It was a courtyard! From the doors, a red brick path wove its way under trellises and vines with beautiful blooming wisteria. The path curved alongside a hill then down to an amphitheatre. The courtyard was shaped like a miniature valley and as my eyes followed the path to the center, I could see people dressed in ballroom attire dancing and there was a band!

Music filled the house. There were birds singing and on the far side of the hill I could see people sitting at tables with elaborate picnics spread before them. There were adults and children, turned out in spring finery as if it were Easter. The aromas that filled my nostrils were overwhelming. I could smell pastries, perfume and food cooking on an open fire. As I turned to see Claudia's reaction, the warm breeze carried a butterfly over and it landed in her hair. It was the most beautiful butterfly I had ever seen. It was mostly yellow, with lines of black, red and purple. Claudia was taking it all in and was standing mesmerized, the butterfly in her hair. I knew I would never have another love like this one in my mortal life. What a crazy ironic world. Nothing is perfect but there are perfect moments that are etched in our heads forever and this was one of them.

I knew what I must do next but had no intention of cutting this moment short. When she noticed me staring at her, she smiled without looking at me, intoxicated by sensory overload. As she slowly turned her head the butterfly lit from her shoulder and fluttered ever so gently to my shoulder. The slow motion made me feel as if I was in a cloud and everything was drifting. I looked at Claudia and our eyes met, our hands still joined, just taking it all in.

"Babes are you coming home? Mommy misses you," I heard from my right ear exactly where the butterfly had landed. It sounded like my mother.

She was the only one who called me "babes." I had been here so long, I almost didn't recognize her voice. From the bottom of my feet, I felt tingling that ran to the top of my head and my hair felt as if it was standing on end. I suddenly had a flash of memory that happened so fast I instantly recalled all the moments since my arrival here. The next thought that ran through my mind was of being homesick. The second it entered my head, I knew I had to get rid of it before the house could pick up on our plan.

Suddenly I knew it was time. It was now or never. I had to go and so did Claudia.

But, it was too late. I turned to look at her as her trance broke and her face changed. Her eyes opened wide and she screamed at the top of her lungs, "Andy!"

The butterfly had suddenly changed to a tarantula, the room went dark and a dreadfully cold wind picked up. Claudia was not looking at the transformed butterfly, but past me. She shrieked even louder again and lost her grip on my hand as she reflexively covered her mouth. I turned to see vines quickly coming from the basement along the walls. They were growing along the floor as well and I knew they were coming after me. We had no time to run to the stairs. Our only option was to go toward the courtyard. I somehow knew I should not go there; it was not my place to be, yet.

"Claudia you have to go now or you will be trapped here forever! Remember what we talked about," I yelled.

"I will be fine. You're my forever angel. Now run! Please!"

I screamed, fearing for her safety more than mine.

"Come with me Andy. You can't stay here. The house will destroy you," she said frantically. She knew I was going to stay and fight.

I looked over my shoulder and realized the moment had come to face my own destiny. The house was furious and I was as well, at myself. I had been worried about Claudia spilling the beans and in the end I was the one who ultimately didn't control my thoughts. I would not be so hard on myself later, I knew, as I could never deny the sound of my mother's voice. She was my world and I would never turn away from her, if I could help it. But for now I was responsible for letting my emotions slip at the last moment and my Claudia was in danger of never seeing her destination. I was ready to fight and was not going to let fear ruin this moment!

As the vines began to surround us, it was obvious that they did not want us to go toward the gardens. The house did not want us to leave and was going to stop us, even if it had to destroy us and itself in the process. From above came a roar so loud that it shook the chandelier violently, and it began swaying. Then there was another roar. A high-pitched, piercing squealing from the gargoyles echoing above us. The house was unleashing all of its beasts at once. The chandelier started twisting as a funnel cloud began to form above it. The sound of the storm and the beasts in tandem was deafening.

It was all happening too fast. I remembered how much mind control I had in this place and tried to focus on what needed to be done.

"Claudia, this is your last chance. You have to go, NOW!" I pleaded. I reached for her and put my hand around her neck, pulling her face to mine and gave her a kiss. I paused to look closely into her eyes and that moment seemed like minutes, not seconds. I knew it would be the last time I would ever see her again. She was crying, but managed to smile and said, "I will always be watching after you and I will love you forever. Always!"

I was about to reply when the vines wrapped around my legs. Before my face could hit the floor, I gave Claudia a hard push towards the courtyard, so hard she tripped in that direction, almost losing her balance. As she passed through the doors, there was a hum like the sound from a power pole transformer, then crackling as static electricity sparked across the threshold. It was clearly visible that there was a force field in the doorway. Sparks and light flew everywhere and I heard a final zap as she made it to the other side.

My synapses had just enough time to register a scene from a Star Trek episode and that brought a confident, rebellious grin to my face. Claudia had made it!

Meanwhile, I had gained much confidence and had taken enough emotional abuse from this house and was ready to stand my ground. I was not going to go down without a fight!

Claudia regained her balance on the other side and turned to me screaming, "Master Andy!"

She was crying in desperation. "You leave him alone!" she cursed the house. She was not wielding her usual rage. Her powers must have been useless there, in paradise. She deserved that place. She was free and I was grateful for that. I noticed that she had the look of a normal mortal girl and all her ghostly features had disappeared. She was not aware but a man and woman were approaching her from behind. It must have been her parents who had been waiting so long to be reunited with their daughter.

I was about to reply when the vines ran up my legs and I was slammed to the floor as they pulled me back toward my original point of entry into the house — the cellar. The winds were wild and I could barely see the chandelier twisting inside the tornado; the bolts in the ceiling wincing from their mounts. A funnel cloud formed above me and blew open the door that must have lead to the balcony on the roof. The funnel cloud started working its way to the floor increasing speed. The chandelier began winding up as it was twisted clockwise taking everything around me with it. "At least I am going to be killed from the chandelier before being eaten by the lions," I thought.

As I was being dragged off my feet by the vines, I heard mother's crying again, "Son, please come back to me. I miss you."

With one last shred of hope that I would not be killed

or doomed to the same long imprisonment as my sweet Claudia, I screamed at the top of my lungs, "I want to go home!" The wind picked me up off the ground and I was being spun like a top, the vines winding tighter around my legs. The pain was excruciating. By now I was at least ten feet off the ground and I was about to be sucked into the twister. Below I could see the lions coming toward me but I was rising quickly. I had the opportunity to catch one last glimpse of Claudia standing there behind the gates of Paradise. She was crying for me with her hands over her mouth. Her parents each had a hand on her shoulders but she was not acknowledging them. She was screaming for me.

"I love you Claudia. I love you mother. I will miss you both!" I screamed and as soon as the words escaped, bright lights emanated from my mouth and I felt a surge of energy like an electric shock. It didn't feel like rage or fear but pure love; it was like a river of energy flowing out of me. As I screamed, the whole house shook. The chandelier finally broke free and was falling towards me.

Home

"Where do you think she is right now?" Steve asked, his eyes wide open and staring at me in half disbelief and half incredible wonder.

"Heaven of course," I replied. "It was her version of heaven and I hope my heaven is that beautiful when I go there someday."

As we sat on our rock, the outpost on top of the hill overlooking our secret cabin, and I finished the story, Steve was now drilling me with questions. His excitement was uncontrollable.

"Damn, Andy! That was unbelievable," he exclaimed. "I believe every word but it is so hard to imagine. When you woke up and saw your mother there, what happened? How did you feel? What did you remember happening right before you awoke from the coma? Did the chandelier fall on you? You were only away from us in your head for two days, but it must have seemed like months."

"As the winds and vines wrapped around me and I saw the Chandelier falling towards me, I heard my mother calling and everything went bright. The only thing I could see was white light but I could hear her voice. Then, I saw a shadow in front of me. Just before I regained my focus, I heard Claudia speaking in a soft voice, ever so content, 'Master Andy, you did it. We are free and safe now. I will always love you and miss you. Now go be with Miss Sarah and tell her Claudia says hello.' Then I woke up and my mother was by the hospital bed weeping and holding my hand. She had been there the whole time waiting for me to return."

"I could still feel my heart beating furiously when I awoke and didn't know where I was. My mother said I sat straight up in bed, wide eyed screaming Claudia's name. While I was in the coma, time sort of stopped. I could not tell night from day. Imagine how Claudia felt. It was like living another life. It was like eternity."

Steve just sat there looking at the ground; his eyes still wide with amazement. He did not want to disbelieve me, but it was so hard to swallow: Lions and gargoyles, tunnels and secret passageways, a dead girl and ghosts. He smiled after a moment and asked with a tone of hesitation in his voice, "So are you ready to go back there to claim your treasure? It's been a week since you left the hospital. I'm surprised you haven't gone back yet."

I paused, recalling it all. I could still see Claudia's face as she stood on the threshold of heaven crying. I missed her so much. I was hesitant to go back because I was still a bit afraid of the house. I still had the desire to collect my treasure but now, somehow it didn't seem as important as it did before. After all, it was a physical object; replaceable. But there was only one Claudia and I knew that when I returned I would be looking for her. I was not ready to face that yet.

"The wildest thing about the whole experience is the letter my mother wrote," I said to Steve with a heavy heart, holding back tears. "I haven't been able to tell mom yet. I am afraid to tell her. If she says she never met Claudia and didn't write the letter, then I will have to face the fact that maybe Claudia was only in my head. I am not ready to let her go yet. I may never be ready. I love her, Steve, as crazy as that may sound. My first love was a ghost, how funny is that?" I said choking back the tears. "She was smart, pretty and sensitive and she also had tenacity. She stood up for me and she loved me as well. I cannot let her go inside my head or heart. She will always be a part of me and I am not ready to tell mom. If she says she didn't write the letter, then she will think I am crazy if I tell her about Claudia. Steve just sat there staring blankly into nowhere. He didn't need to comment. Most anyone would find all this hard to believe just as many find it hard to believe in God or heaven. But I experienced it and Steve did not want to discredit me or show his lack of faith either. He just sat there looking at me as I confessed everything.

He was a true friend. Like my father always said, a true friend is hard to find. If you have one or two true friends in life you are lucky. A true friend just wants you to be happy. Steve's lack of feedback was welcome at this moment. It meant that he didn't want to burst my bubble. I knew he wanted to see the Big House and now he was dying to go there. He trusted me that when I was ready, we would go.

He looked up at me and smiled.

"You are lucky, Master Andy," Steve chuckled. "You found love, mystery adventure and even proof of heaven. And no one will ever take that from you." He winked.

The sound of branches cracking behind us broke the spell. All three of the Hopkins boys had snuck behind the rock, circling from behind us, catching us by surprise. Eugene stepped up to the rock, his head and shoulders just above where our feet were dangling from the boulder.

"So, you didn't learn your lesson the last time I see," Eugene said with contempt. "Steve, you should know better. He doesn't belong here. He is one rich kid in a big house and this is our turf. You are just a kiss-ass."

"Am not, "Steve retorted. "Andy is cool. It isn't his fault he lives there. He's my friend. Maybe if you just took some time to know him, you would see he's a good kid. Besides, this isn't your woods and you don't own us."

Bobby whispered something to Johnny and they laughed.

"What the hell are you laughing about?" Eugene snarled at the others.

"I guess they didn't learn their lesson the last time is all I said," Bobby replied stuttering slightly. "Maybe they need a reminder."

"Yeah, maybe," Eugene replied, turning to us and grimacing, clenching his fists and pounding one into the other repeatedly.

"You have one more shot to get the hell out of here in one piece. Now!" he commanded as he turned his intimidating gaze to me.

"We're taking over this fort and now that we know where your secret cabin is, you have nowhere else to go. Now beat it before I kick both of your asses."

Steve slid down from the rock and looked back up at me. I knew he just wanted to keep the peace and since he lived in the same place with them he must conform or they would never give him any peace. He just stared at me for a second, expecting me to follow and when I didn't budge, he lowered his brow and jerked his head left, indicating that I should do the same and scram.

As Steve stood there, giving me the signal to run or leave before they started any more trouble, my mind was somewhere else. I recalled the moments in the Big House and all the adventures, thrills and terror that I had experienced if even in my head. Claudia and I had stood up to so many threats from the house. It sort of made this situation feel like child's play, although I knew that this was the real world and if Eugene and his henchmen wanted to, they could kick our asses and would definitely do so if we didn't obey them.

Even so, after all I had experienced, the situation today seemed so trivial, unthreatening and almost comical. Things were different now, at least for me.

I was surprised that I was not the least bit intimidated.

Plus, I truly believed I had a secret weapon: my angel, my Claudia. If I believed in her and the house and all that happened then, I had to believe she was indeed watching over me now and would help me and Steve.

Again, here was another of those moments in life when you have to choose. Either do as they say and bow down, letting them continue their rule over me or stand up and face my fears, but at least do something to defend myself. I decided to do the latter. Steve was getting nervous and just wanted to avoid conflict especially after the last episode where I was knocked unconscious.

"Come on Andy let's get out of here," he said, pleading.

I closed my eyes just for a moment and whispered, "Love is the key and the key is love."

"What did you say you little twerp?" Eugene asked.

"He said, 'I need another ass kicking,'" snapped Johnny.

I looked Eugene straight in the eye, showing no fear, smiled and very politely replied in an English accent, "No I think not. This is our fort and we are not leaving. Perhaps you should leave before we kick the bloody hell out of you three."

Steve's mouth dropped and he flinched, his fight or flight instinct kicking in. He was ready to run. He just looked at Eugene waiting for his response, frozen beside me.

"OK, I guess you need another reminder of who's in charge here you spoiled little brat," Eugene said as he reached forward to grab my dangling feet off the boulder.

I had no time to pull my legs back and he grabbed me by the ankles and pulled, scraping my back as I was dragged down the rock. My head bounced off the rock and I landed on the ground. Sparks of electricity went through my body to my fingers, obviously from the slight agitation to my healing head. This time it felt familiar and welcoming. "I heard you got knocked out for a few days. This time you may not be so lucky," he threatened. Steve was about to step in to defend me as Eugene balled up his fist ready to start pounding me.

"No!" I commanded Steve. "I will handle this," I said, slightly shaky but fully intending to follow through with the confrontation. My whole body was tingling but this time not out of fear. I remembered how Claudia had stood up for me as we were escaping the secret passageway and all the moments when I had to stand up to my fears as I faced the unknown perils inside the Big House. We trusted ourselves despite the fear and somehow made it back to where we needed to be.

We survived. I would survive this too. Steve was always defending me and I would take a beating for him this time if I had to. My adrenaline was pumping and I felt the same way I always do in these trying moments; a little like stage fright. But I felt it would pass just like every other moment I had recently endured, trusting that it would be no more different here as in the other world. On this day, with the strength I had gained through my friendship with Steve, and my love for Claudia, I stood up to Eugene and his brothers.

Eugene, who was at least two feet taller than me, smirked at me and mocked, "So. You'll handle this, will 'ya?"

I was shaking and scared but ready for this moment, as ready as I would ever be and I could not allow myself to stand down.

I looked at Steve and winked, remembering that last wink from Claudia before we parted forever. Steve's mouth had dropped and he stepped back a bit not knowing if he could defend me now that I was being so defiant.

"Do you wanna take a trip to the other side? It's a lotta fun and a very wild ride, a very wild ride," I sang out loud with a smile on my face, my eyes focused on Eugene. I was interrupted by a sharp pain as Eugene wielded his best swing and cracked me in the jaw.

"Hold him, so I can teach him a lesson he will never forget," he grunted at the other two. They grabbed my arms and slammed me up against the rock, pinning me.

The initial fear and pain had gone and was replaced with that familiar tingling, numb vibration throughout my head. It felt like it did when the key resonated through my body. I had gotten past that first moment and had taken my first step past the fear. The worst was over. My head was down and lolling around my shoulders from the first blow. Still I kept mumbling my made up song.

"Come on Eugene, don't do this again. He's had enough abuse from you all. Let him go and we won't come back again," Steve pleaded.

That in itself outraged me. Steve had always defended me and it wasn't fair for either of us. Eugene balled his fist again, reared back for another hard punch and I just looked up at him and grimaced.

Before he could take his best shot, I looked him straight in the eyes and shouted, "Not this time!" He paused and the other two just stared my way in shock. My eyes were burning with rage, remorse and revenge, but more so, I thought of Claudia and in a split second I felt her hand in mine. I flexed my arms free from the boys, and felt the lightening course through my body and pass from my arms to them, and they went airborne, rolling down the hill, as we watched them hitting rocks along the way down. Blood was gushing from Eugene's forehead as he reached solid ground.

I could not break my gaze from Eugene. His whole persona changed from dominating to petrified. I heard Steve say softly, "Oh my God."

My eyes were glowing red hot like Claudia's when she saved us from the wolves. I knew it wasn't me alone summoning this power. My guardian angel was here with me!

Before I could allow myself to retaliate and break Eugene down into pieces, I remembered how the house responded when I was not so afraid of it. It shared all the same emotions Claudia and I had shared and it only got angry when it was afraid of being alone.

All of a sudden Eugene didn't seem so mean and threatening and I almost felt sorry for him.

It wasn't his fault that he was born into these conditions: less than adequate housing, parenting and love. Life wasn't fair. And what kind of person would I be if I punished him like he did me, even though I didn't deserve it. My eyes were blazing and the rage subsided only slightly as I was still feeling vengeful if for no other reason than what this was doing to Steve. I managed to replace that empowered feeling with just enough empathy that I held back my desire to crush Eugene for all the pain he had inflicted on me.

We descended the hill and reached them, and I grabbed him by the throat and opened my mouth, "I have had enough!" I bellowed and when I did the light steamrolled from my mouth and the heat and wind blew back his hair and turned his face red. Steve and the others were standing there unable to make a sound, frozen by fear and amazement. "You will leave here now and will not come back unless invited. If you do, I will destroy you. If you decide that you can treat Steve and myself with a little respect then maybe, just maybe we can start over and get along. For now, get lost!" I reiterated with fury in the form of blinding light and ear-popping sound. "I am not your enemy, but if that is your wish, I can be. Now leave, run and don't look back."

Before I could finish, the other two punks were scrambling to their feet and running at top speed tripping over logs and rocks in a desperate attempt to get as far as they could from me.

"Do you understand?" I asked Eugene. "We can get along, but you better start treating people nicer or else I will treat you like you have others. I do not like violence but if that is the way you want to play, so be it. Now Cheerio!" I said with a final threatening grimace.

I loosened my grip, not realizing that I had raised him off the ground. He fell to his knees as they were not able to respond quickly enough from the drop. He scrambled to his feet and was off running. I could hear him breathing and whimpering as if he was a scared little baby.

I calmed myself and took a deep breath. When I finally looked over at Steve, his mouth was still open but he had a look of utter disbelief. He broke into a smile as if he could not believe he had won the lottery.

"Where the hell did that come from?" he gasped. " I would ask if you are OK but obviously you can hold your own. Dude, that was freaky," he said. You just became a monster!"

"They brought out the best in me, I guess. Besides I have a guardian angel now." I looked up to the sky and smiled. Claudia would have been proud of me. Just then a butterfly lit on my shoulder from out of nowhere. It had the same colors and markings. I knew it was not all my doing. She was there for me just as I was for her. I just stared at it as it took flight then looked over at Steve and smiled.

He somehow understood.

"Now that we're free of those bullies, Steve, what do you say we go on a little adventure and visit the Big House? Who knows, maybe we'll run into Claudia."

Steve paused for a moment. "I'm not sure I want to go now. That was scary, man. I want to come back alive. I don't want to get eaten by a house, wolves or lions."

He was still shaken and maybe even a little afraid of me at this moment. I was not as proud of myself as he was but I was thankful that obviously, I had brought something back from the Big House. Even if mom denied having ever meeting Claudia, I was convinced it had all really happened.

"Trust me," I said. "The house is at peace now and besides we have someone looking over us. Along the way, I need to stop and ask mom if it is OK. She shouldn't mind. She knows nothing about the house and what I saw. I have to get my treasure. And maybe you can meet Claudia. You both would like each other. She is awesome."

Although Steve was still in shock from what he had just seen, we were friends and had the ultimate trust. We started walking, his hands on his head trying to digest what had just happened. We walked back around the lookout rock for the fort and I started singing a song making it up as I went. Steve laughed out loud and hummed along as we walked back to our bikes. I looked at him and for a second his eyes took on a green glow that I had seen before.

"Naw," I pretended to deny it was possible. But, you never know where spirits go. I was just happy to have my best friend by my side and Claudia forever in my heart.

A Message From the Author

Hope is the little engine we all rely upon to keep our spirit alive. That combined with adventure is the secret to fulfillment. Along the road of life we all have trials and tribulations that keep us in check, help us grow and become wise.

We all go through the motions, feeling these highs and lows, and it is OK to be vulnerable at times. Life's little lessons are that basis of who are, where we are going and who we will become. Endure the pain, embrace the love of family and friends and by all means share. Without sharing we are alone and left without much zest for enduring.

There is only one "you". Embrace yourself and others will embrace you as well. Stand tall even despite the falls!

No fear!

Thank you for reading **The Big House**. Your feedback, criticism, and praise are appreciated.

Robert Vasvary

Robert Vasvary is an electrical engineer and avid boatsman who lives happily with his wife and son in Boca Raton, Florida. He can often be found in Quito, Ecuador, where his wife's family resides. **The Big House** is the first book in a series. **Circles of Harmony**, the second Big House book, will be available in early 2015.

For more information, visit the bighousebook.com
To purchase the book or ebook visit robertvasvary.com

To write the author, agent or publisher contact:
info@thebighousebook.com

To contact the editor or illustrator email:
info@firewatercreative.net

All characters appearing in Robert Vasvary's THE BIG HOUSE series of books are fictitious. Any resemblance to real persons, living or dead, is purely coincidental and possibly laughable.

The Big House
"The Beginning"

stay tuned in 2015 for the second
Andy Miller series

The Big House
"Circles of Harmony"
by Robert Vasvary